OTHER BOOKS BY EDIE RAMER

Contemporary
MUST WORSHIP CATS (a Miracle Interrupted novella)
STARDUST MIRACLE (a Miracle Interrupted novel)
MIRACLE LANE (a Miracle Interrupted novel)
MIRACLE PIE (a Miracle Interrupted novel)
MO'S HEART (a Miracle Interrupted novel)
YOU'VE GOT MURDER co-written with Karin Tabke

Paranormal
CATTITUDE
DEAD PEOPLE
DEAD PEOPLE IN LOVE (short story)
DRAGON BLUES
THE SEVENTH DIMENSION (short story)

Science Fiction Romance
GALAXY GIRLS
MIXING IT UP (a Galaxy Girls novella)

Short Stories and Essays
The Fat Cat in ENTANGLED, A PARANORMAL
ANTHOLOGY
(all proceeds go to Breast Cancer Research Foundation)
The Kiss in EVERY WITCH WAY BUT WICKED
(all proceeds go to Kids Need to Read)
Killing the Rat Bastard Disease in AUTHOR MOMENTS
Fighting Back in AUTHOR MOMENTS II
(all proceeds of the Author Moments books go to Cancer
Research UK)

For updates, go to http://edieramer.com

Miracle
Pie

A Miracle Interrupted novel

Edie Ramer

Blue Walrus Books

~o~

A miracle is prophesied in a small village...
And everyone secretly believes
it's meant for them.

~o~

ONE

Need spiraled inside Katie Guthrie as she reached her cottage, her morning pie deliveries done, her headlights slicing through the gloomy dawn, her windshield wipers slapping up and down. She ran inside, not caring that she was getting damp, and tossed her jacket at a hook in the back hall. It fell to the floor, and she left it. She needed to do this *now* and do it *fast*.

She jerked cupboard doors open and grabbed ingredients. The urgency more intense than usual. *Now, now, now. Hurry, hurry, hurry.* She felt like a contestant on a TV cooking show. As if it were a do or die moment.

It's just pie, she told herself, but it didn't stop her from jerking open the refrigerator door and grabbing the heavy whipping cream. She headed to her mixer on the counter. Whoever it was meant for would be here soon.

The pie was never wrong.

Katie gaped at Rosa Fabrini, standing in her kitchen with raindrops glistening on her luxuriant hair. The shapely matriarch's dark brown eyes were like bruises today, her normal high-voltage charisma ebbed as if she were a toy in need of recharging.

Shock froze Katie's voice. This must be a mistake. Someone else must be coming soon for the pie in her refrigerator that was just reaching perfection.

A snore came from the living room where Happy, Katie's old, nearly deaf and blind Beagle, slept. No doubt dreaming that one of Katie's pies would miraculously fall off the counter and she'd eat it all. *No reason for Mom to clean. I'm a good dog. I'll take care of it.*

"I'm leaving Mike," Rosa said.

A shockwave slammed through Katie. Rosa and Mike had been married as long as Katie could remember. Their sons were almost the same age as her. This was not good.

Or was it?

Seconds passed while she wondered what to say.

It's about time.

You can do better than that asshole.

I want to do a happy dance.

None of those words came out of her mouth. Instead she made a low sound of sympathy, stepped forward and hugged the woman she'd often wished had been her mother. Rosa collapsed on Katie's shoulder.

This was her second friend who was in trouble. The other one lived in California. A long drive from Wisconsin. Katie gave Rosa an extra squeeze. *This is for you, too, Trish. I hope you can feel it.*

"It's going to be okay." Katie patted Rosa's damp hair as if she were Happy or her father's rescue dog, Puck. It *should* be okay, she thought. Rosa deserved to have a good life.

And Mike... Well, he deserved a good kick in his self-important, cheating ass.

Rosa sniffed and pulled away. "I got you wet."

"No, you didn't," Katie lied. Now that she'd lost Rosa's body warmth, she shivered. September had hit Wisconsin with a record heat wave just a week ago, but today the rain had brought cold air.

And a friend in need.

Maybe Katie didn't know what to say, but she knew what to do. "Sit down. I have an Everything Will Get Better Pie in the fridge."

Rosa's laugh came out as a half sob. She grasped Katie's arm, stopping her. "I can't eat."

"You'll feel better after you eat my pie." People *always* felt better after they ate her pies. She'd heard that since she baked her first pie while under the direction of her grandmother when she was barely six years old. As if a fairy had given her a gift at birth, her gram used to say. The gift of pie.

When her dad heard about the prophecy of a miracle at church last spring, he'd said, *"Every pie you make is a miracle."*

"I'm not here for pie." Rosa grasped Katie's arm, and Katie turned back to her. Katie was five nine, and Rosa an inch or so shorter but with so much presence she often seemed *more* than everyone around her. Right now her dark eyes burned into Katie's. "I'm not here for pity, either. I have an idea."

Katie stared at Rosa. She wasn't good at these guessing games. Some people were good at subtext, but Katie saved her subtext for putting just the right amount of seasoning in her pies.

"The pie is creamy chocolate." Katie could hear her voice change, turning dreamlike, her forehead muscles relaxing. That's how pie affected her. Her own precious prayer to make the world better, one pie at a time. "It starts with a rich, dark chocolate bottom, then a mix of mascarpone and heavy cream for the middle. The top is heavy whipped cream with chocolate curls."

She should have known it was meant for Rosa. All the

ingredients pointed to her. In Katie's mind, she pictured Rosa sitting at her table taking a bite, then licking her lips to make sure she didn't miss a dollop of the topping, the tension in her face replaced with bliss. She could hear Rosa saying, *"You know I was too good for him."* Katie's pie making the revelation as clear as water.

And Katie would reply, *"Everyone knows that."*

Which was the truth. Thanks mostly to Linda Wegner at Wegner's, the village store that carried food, diapers, flashlights, batteries, books, sundries and the latest gossip, everyone in the village of Miracle knew about Mike's wandering eyes and hands. Not to mention the body part below his belt.

If someone shopped elsewhere, there was always Angie Schuster at Le Curl (We Do Men Too!), who talked longer and more in depth to make up for not being first. Katie supposed it must be hard to be second in one's favorite activity.

Not that Katie knew about that. No one made pies as good as hers.

It wasn't something she was particularly proud of. She'd never strived for this talent, it just was. There were child prodigies at most arts. Her art was making perfect pies.

"Eat my pie and tell me about the idea," she said.

"If I eat a piece of your pie, I might want to eat the whole thing."

"Then eat the whole thing."

Rosa laughed and shook her head, but her laughter was like burnt popcorn pieces popping into the air. "You won't relax until I eat, will you?"

Katie touched Rosa's upper arm. "It's okay. Forget the pie. Tell me first." Rosa needed to spit out the bad taste inside her before she could enjoy anything. Katie knew what that was like. "What happened?"

"Amber's pregnant." Rosa's rich voice was flat.

A hot flush of anger took away the chill on Katie's skin. "Mike's the father?"

Rosa nodded. "He didn't tell me. She did."

"Coward."

"*Bastardo.*"

"That too. You're really leaving him?"

"I leave him or I kill him." Her lips bared, Rosa looked up and shook her fists at the ceiling, as if at God. "How dare he do this? How dare he?"

Katie didn't answer, though she could guess why Mike cheated. He was a weak man, and weak men needed to convince themselves they were strong. They thought putting their penis in places it didn't belong was the best proof. It was something they could silently gloat over to make them feel good.

I did that, they thought. *I had sex with her. That proves I'm strong and virile.*

Katie knew about weak people. Her mother had been like that, dropping Katie off at her dad's like an unwanted package when she was five.

"You're better off without him," Katie said, bringing her attention back to Rosa. "Will you still work at the restaurant?"

"Never!" Rosa's voice rang out. "I want to have my own cooking show. I've wanted it for a long time, but Mike said there was too much competition."

Katie nodded because that led back to her first conclusion. In addition to the wandering penis and dictator imitations, weak men were afraid of competition. That's why Fabrini's Fine Italian Dining was located in a small village instead of New York City or Chicago. Mike was a big-fish-in-a-tiny-pond kind of guy.

He certainly wouldn't want Rosa to be the star. He wouldn't want to take the chance that she'd outshine him.

"You'll be a great TV cook," Katie said. "You're beautiful, sexy, funny and a wonderful cook."

Rosa's mouth straightened and she seemed to pull inward and stand taller. "I'm not as young as I once was."

"No one is as young as they once were. You're only, what, forty-something?"

"Forty-something will do."

"Whatever, you're still gorgeous. You'll be gorgeous when you're in your sixties. In your eighties, even."

Rosa's shoulders relaxed and she laughed, low and throaty. She patted Katie's cheek. "You're good for my heart." She glanced past her at the kitchen. "And you'll be good for my cooking show."

"You want me to do prep work?" Katie's stomach tightened. She supposed she could find time from her pie making business, but only if Rosa filmed the show in Miracle.

"We'll be a team." Rosa motioned with both hands. "You're young and attractive, and you have a good figure. More important, you make wonderful pies. I'll demonstrate how to make Italian food, and you demonstrate how you make pies."

"You want me to be on your show?" Katie heard her voice rise into a squeak. "I'm too tall and gangly." Like a tall ship floundering in the ocean, a friend's cousin from Eau Claire had said when she was fifteen. For weeks afterward, she'd tried to walk like the other girls. Small steps instead of long, fast strides that took her to her objective.

She finally realized she didn't want to change. Her walk reflected who she was.

At least she wasn't one person lost in a crowd of look-alikes.

And she wasn't on TV, either.

"You need to find someone else."

TWO

Oh oh. Katie took a step back and crossed her arms, as if they could ward off the look Rosa was giving her. The one her sons called The Stare.

"I remember when you first came to Miracle," Rosa said. "I came to the farm to pick up eggs. Your dad was so proud of you. If someone had given him a choice of you or a diamond the size of his fist, he wouldn't have given the diamond a second glance."

Katie closed her eyes, the memories rushing back. Giving her a warm ache.

"You were so quiet and shy," Rosa continued. "And me with two rambunctious little boys. I was so jealous of Sam. I hugged you and whispered that you were the prettiest girl. You looked at me with your eyes wide and round, as if you didn't believe it. All these years later, you still have that same lost look."

Katie snapped her eyelids up. "I have a wonderful life."

"Yes, like a swaddled baby. You're not taking risks. You're not moving beyond your comfort zone."

"I like my comfort zone. I'm happy in it."

Rosa looked at her pityingly. "The problem with comfort zones is that they keep shrinking, and after a while you shrink with them."

"My business is doing really well." Katie crossed her arms. She wasn't used to defending her choices and didn't like it.

"I'm just doing a pilot," Rosa said, her voice compelling. "It might be just a onetime thing. If I don't sell it to any TV stations, I won't make anymore." Her gaze held Katie's. "That's why I need you to help make it a success. A show with two women will get more attention. And to be honest, I need your kitchen."

Katie glanced around at the shining industrial kitchen that her dad had built after her grandmother had gone on to the much bigger cottage in the sky.

"I know I'm being selfish—" Rosa's voice cracked and her shoulders slumped. She sighed. "Never mind. I'll find another way. It's wrong to try to bully you into it."

She started to turn away, and Katie felt ashamed for making such a drama. Sure, she baked pies for friends, but that was as easy for her as breathing. If she couldn't handle a little discomfort to help Rosa out of a dark spot in her life, that meant she wasn't much of as friend.

"Okay, I'll do it. But if I really hate it or I'm awful, I won't do any more."

Rosa swung back, a smile lighting up her face as if she'd just won a Powerball lottery. "Wonderful! And you'll be stupendous."

"Don't get too excited." Katie frowned. "I don't have your charisma. You're perfect for a show like that. You have magic inside you."

"You have magic in your pies."

"The viewers won't be eating my pies. They'll be watching me make them."

"Don't devalue yourself." Rosa stood with her spine straight, like a soldier ready for battle. "We are women, and we are fabulous. Men should be lucky they have us."

"If you say so. Will you have my pie now?"

"It will be my pleasure." Rosa swung her hands out.

"Your pies are ambrosia. Food of the Gods."

Rosa went on to say she was calling the producer-director, a nephew of someone she knew. Nodding, Katie took the pie out of the fridge. In its glass pie plate, she saw the layers of chocolate and cream topping. Just looking at it, without even taking a bite, she felt a transfusion of energy. As if it was sending out waves of love and vitality.

Katie hoped they were heading straight to Rosa who was at the table already, the cell phone to her ear as she talked, her voice low and intense. At the counter, Katie cut the pie while Rosa perched on a chair, still talking, her face animated, her brown eyes glowing. Katie brought the pie and forks to the table.

"Just one pilot," Rosa was saying. "If it works out, when I sell it I'll see if you can film them. Once you get here, we can talk some more."

There was silence for a moment, then Rosa gave him her address and hung up. "He'll be here in two days."

Katie sat across from Katie, not saying anything. She wasn't sure how she felt about this.

Rosa picked up the fork, the expression on her face different now. Ravenous. As if she'd been starved for days. For years. As if the pie symbolized all the good that she'd missed.

She chewed the first bite with her lids down and a look of bliss on her face. When she swallowed, she opened her eyes. "That was like biting into a tiny piece of heaven."

Katie's body hummed with quiet contentment, and she took another bite of her pie.

"You know what this pie tells me?" Rose shook her fork at her plate.

"That a good pie is worth more than a bad husband?"

Rosa laughed. "It's probably true, but it tells me that life is still filled with delicious possibilities, and I can do anything I set my mind on doing."

Katie used the side of her fork to cut off another piece. "My pies are very smart."

"But that's not all it tells me."

Katie raised her eyebrows. "And my pies are talkative."

"It's the truth." Rosa raised her fork with a bite of pie into the air, as if in a salute. "It's telling me that both our lives are going to change for the better." Only then did Rosa take a second bite, her gaze still on Katie.

Katie shivered with a chill she felt in her gut. Changes were like chain reactions. Once they started, anything could happen. Including blowing up in their faces.

THREE

Shoving his Chicago Bears sweatshirt in the suitcase as fast as he could, Gabe thought in song titles: *Breaking Up is Hard to Do* even when it was never *True Love* but *Just One of Those Things*.

Too bad *One of Those Things* wanted to kick him in a vulnerable spot right now.

"You. Can't. Fucking. Do. This." Cherise stood over him in the condo they shared that had almost a Lake Michigan view. A tiny blue slice out the front window that gave Cherise bragging rights.

He continued to pack though the air shuddered with her vibrations of anger. With her shiny black hair coiled tightly in a bun and her even tighter body, she made Gabe think of a stripper about to shake her hair loose then tear off her pencil skirt and matching top as she strutted across a stage.

Only that hadn't happened in the three years he'd known her and the eleven months he'd lived with her.

If it had, she might not be so easy to leave. He was after all, a man, and was shallow that way.

Then he thought of the picture of the two women his uncle sent him. The older one with the body that Gabe's uncle called "va-va-voom" was fully dressed but his uncle was right about her curves. And her face had a strong bone structure that would appeal to women as well as men. The younger one, with startled eyes, parted lips, and brown hair pulled up in a ponytail, made him think of a mermaid stranded on dry land.

His uncle always had great taste.

"Aren't you going to answer me?" Cherise asked, her tone edged with anger.

Focus. He needed to focus. He glanced over his shoulder. "I'm just going to talk to them."

"To two women." She spat out the three words like they were a bad wine.

He straightened and turned around. "This is nothing to do with them. I'd already given you notice."

"You were still going to do jobs for me."

"Once in a while." Until he found his missing mojo. His magic. His passion for life. Lost for four years now. Too long to be floundering around according to his understanding mom, stepdad and father. Too long for him, too.

"You're making good money with me," she said. "My work is steady, which is more than most filmmakers can say. What are you looking for that I don't have?"

"My place in the sun." He kept his tone light when all he wanted to do was leave. "My niche in life."

Cherise rolled her eyes at the ten-foot ceiling. "*Niche?* Antique stores have niches. Little old ladies have niches. You need a plan or you'll never get anywhere."

"These last couple years I've been helping you with your dream. You always knew that when I found my dream, I'd—"

"I have a *plan*, not a dream." She crossed her arms, the air around her glacial with icy spikes of anger. "Dreams are for dreamers. Plans are for doers."

He ached for her for being so wrong and so cold. For not believing in dreams.

And he ached for himself, for staying with her while

he waited for a dream that never showed up.

Until now. Not a full-fledged dream, but a glimmer. Bright and shiny, calling his name.

"Maybe you're right." He turned back to his packing. "But I'm still leaving."

"I have a wedding 7in two days, and you won't be back in time to film it."

"I recommended two good videographers. We've used them both before and they've done good work."

"But they're not *you*. You have a way of calming people down. Making them do what you want, even if it's not what they want."

"Now you're trying to make me do what I don't want to do." He glanced up and met her glittering gaze. "Making my own films was always my goal."

Her mouth pursed and her forehead tightened. "You and about fifty thousand other wannabe filmmakers."

"True, but I'm ready to give it a go now. You knew from the first time you booked me to film a wedding that I had other plans."

"That was three years ago. Since then, you've become more than an employee. You're only leaving now because of the photo your uncle emailed you. Because of *those women*." Her eyes glittered brighter and harder.

He turned away. He couldn't tell her he had no choice. Not since his uncle, who delivered fish to restaurants in the middle of Wisconsin, had sent the pictures of the two women to his cell phone. The moment Gabe looked at them he'd felt a stomach punch and something else...something indescribable. Like when he was seven and dying and a small girl told him angels were going to save him. That he was going to live.

And he did live. Twenty-three years later he was healthy enough for Cherise to consider him as the future father of her children.

She made an angry sound, and he blanked out the images of the girl and the women. Facing Cherise, he saw her as if she was a character in a story he was going to film and this was a scene. Saw the worry and the need to control and the way she took life so seriously.

When life wasn't serious. Life was...wonderful. The first wonder of the world. Living and breathing and walking around on two feet. You just had to open your eyes to it.

Cherise's eyes were wide open, but she didn't see the same things he did. She saw life as a To Do List. He saw life as a To Be Journey.

These last few years he'd forgotten that and he was just starting to remember.

He took her hands in his. Hers were cool and limp.

"My uncle says this woman has *it*."

"*It*." She spat out the word. "What is *it*?"

"Magic. *It* is magic."

She jerked her hands from his. "Your uncle is a horndog, and I don't believe in magic."

"What if I told you magic happened to me? Would you believe then?"

"I would believe you were mentally disturbed."

For a long moment he studied her. She glared back. Defiant. Angry.

A vast sadness was a heavy weight in his chest. Not for him or for her. For *them*. Except there really was no *them*, and there had never been a *them*.

He turned back to the pile of clothes on his bed. He wasn't good at packing—he saved his meticulousness for his work—so he shoved his jeans in the suitcase. He'd already put a few bags of his stuff in his SUV along with his video equipment where most of his money had gone.

EDIE RAMER

"You're taking all your clothes with you?"

"I have a feeling this will work. You know my feelings are usually right."

"With all the talk about feelings, you sound feminine."

"If you're insinuating I might be gay, you should know better." He shifted to look into her eyes. "If I were even bi, I'd tell you. When have you known me to lie?"

Frustration tightened her face. "Maybe I just didn't catch you. You could be a con-man."

"The only money I've taken from you is payment for my videographer services." He even paid for his share of the costs since she'd invited him to move in after the fire at his southside apartment. It was never meant to be permanent. At the time, he'd been glad to have a place to stay.

Now he was glad to leave, though he knew it was her anger talking right now. It wasn't that she loved him. It was just that he was useful, his appearance and manners were acceptable. Best of all, he was low maintenance.

And stubborn. But everyone had a fault, and she was willing to overlook it if only he'd be wise enough to change his mind.

Instead, he packed faster. Five minutes later he stood at the door to the hall with his suitcases.

"If you waltz out of my life," Cherise said, her tone sharp enough to slice through the air, "don't think I'm letting you waltz back in so easily."

"If that's what you want..." He arched his eyebrows.

"I mean it." She flattened her lips into a thin line, her arms pressed against her ribs. No give in her.

The sadness zoomed back to Gabe. This was the woman he'd made love with, slept with, ate with, worked with. He hated to end it this way.

But a feeling about this job was building inside him. An excitement that reminded him of their first vacation together in Puerto Rico when he stood on the edge of a cliff and Cherise pleaded with him not to jump.

He hadn't listened to her then either. The jump had been glorious. He'd felt as if he could fly. It wasn't magic, but close.

Their following two vacations had been to Vegas and Palm Springs to visit Cherise's family. No leaps from cliffs for him anymore. No flying through the air.

No magic.

"We had some good times," he said. But not great. No fierceness. No magic. Just two bodies in proximity using each other.

Her face pulled inward, her nostrils pinched. "You're good in bed, but I want more than that. I want a partner."

Without hesitation, he took his keys out of his pocket and worked one off the ring. Her breaths quickened. Small puffs like an angry cartoon character. Her face twisted in a classic expression of shock.

She hadn't believed he would do it. After three years, she didn't really know him. Didn't know he believed in magic. If he told her, she'd think he was mentally disturbed. But he had to believe in it. After all, magic had happened to him once.

He picked up two suitcases and walked away, hoping that, like lightning, magic would strike twice in the same place.

FOUR

An angel stood in Katie's kitchen next to Rosa. Not the little girl and boy angels on greeting cards. A man. Not much older than her and not much taller, with golden hair, eyes like a summer sky and upturned full lips. Gabriel Robbins even had an angel's name.

Her skin warmed. She couldn't say anything. Not even a greeting. Her voice stuck in her chest, lodged there with her fallen brain cells.

Laughter sparked in his eyes as he said it was nice to meet her. Nothing unusual but his voice wrapped around her like silken strands.

Rosa nudged her arm and still she couldn't speak. She was hyperventilating, her heart pounding, her breaths puffing.

What was wrong with her? He wasn't a movie star. If he were, she suspected she'd be less bemused. She was acting like a schoolgirl instead of a woman who'd had her share of dates and even a couple serious boyfriends. None of them dogs, either—though in four-legged dogs, even ugliness managed to be cute.

This man...he wasn't cute. He wasn't even the most handsome man she'd seen. But he was the most...angelic.

He bent to greet Happy, not seeming to mind that Happy smelled in a way that baths didn't help. An old dog smell that went with Happy's old dog breath.

When Katie finally told Trish about this day, she wouldn't have to exaggerate her social ineptness.

"How old is your dog?" he asked, pulling the long ears gently.

"Happy's nineteen."

"Happy? Good name." Still petting Happy, he gave her a smile that indented dimples in his cheeks.

The inside of her mouth dried up. She shifted her gaze to the bowl of McIntosh apples on her counter that her dad had picked from their own trees. Thoughts of her apple pies brought moistness back to her mouth and her chest opened up, her breathing easier.

"My dad got her when I was eight." Remembering the scampering little pup with the energy of an F-1 tornado, a smile grew inside Katie. "She was the runt of the litter, and no one wanted her. It was either my dad or the humane society."

"She kept you company?"

"What eight-year-old doesn't love a dog?" Especially an eight-year-old who still wondered why her mother didn't keep her.

Boy, did she empathize with that dog.

Of course, being with Sam and her grandma was the best thing that happened to her. Katie knew Happy felt the same way about her.

Gabe gave Happy another scratch behind her ears then straightened and glanced around the kitchen at her two ovens, the KitchenAid mixer, the stainless steel refrigerator and in the corner, her old white one. Then there were the gleaming work spaces. Not the normal cottage kitchen.

She breathed in, feeling double lucky—lucky to have this, and lucky that she remembered just enough of her first five years to appreciate her life now.

"My dad and I redid it two years ago to meet the Board of Health's regulations."

"I like it. A lot of stainless steel."

"Stainless steel is a cook's best friend," she said as she watched Happy limp to the rug in the corner where she slept a good part of the day.

"That and wine," Rosa said, the first she'd spoken since she'd hugged Katie hello.

Gabe laughed low in his throat, more like a devil than an angel. "You ladies are going to be naturals. I can tell already. I have an idea."

Katie groaned. He looked at her, an eyebrow raised. She shrugged. "I heard that same line from Rosa yesterday."

"You're here because of *my* idea." Rosa gave Gabe her I'm-done-with-taking-second-to-a-man look that made his eyebrows rise. "We're all here because of *my* idea. To make *my* show."

Katie restrained herself from patting Rosa on the back and saying *You go, girl.* She knew half of Rosa's determination to do her show was because of Mike. She wanted to be a huge success to make him sorry he'd cheated, though Katie suspected he was already sorry.

But the other half...that was for Rosa.

"It's Rosa's dream," Katie said. That's the real reason she'd said yes to Rosa. She admired people with dreams.

"Not yours?" he asked.

She stepped back and bumped into one of the wooden chairs around the wooden table, an old set that had belonged to her dad's grandmother and then to Katie's grandmother. Plain with no curlicues or notches. Plain just like Katie felt inside.

"I don't need to dream." She peered around, and contentment warmed her insides, like a muffin just out of the oven. "I'm doing exactly what I want. I was eleven when I made my first pie for money. A family friend had lung cancer." She looked at Rosa. "Remember Paul Trilling?"

"A wonderful man."

"He was one of my dad's hunting buddies, and he loved my apple pie." She heard her voice soften. "He said it reminded him of his grandmother's pie."

"Now I remember." Rosa's throaty voice thickened. "Suzie ordered from us, too. The seafood cannelloni." She gestured with her hand, as if Paul and his wife were in the kitchen, watching them. "That's *my* specialty, but Mike claimed the credit. He didn't want me to outshine him. Before Paul's chemo started, Suzie wanted to give him a meal he could remember. We didn't charge her, but she insisted on paying us. She wanted it to be her gift to Paul."

Tears shimmered in her eyes and Katie sniffed her own tears back.

"That's perfect." Gabe's eyes glowed with approval. "I want you to tell this story on your show." He leaned toward both of them. "It's not the cooking that makes people watch a show. It's not even the attractive cooks." He paused, and Katie leaned toward him to hear him better, somehow knowing this important. "It's the story."

"Is that your idea?" Rosa asked. "For us to tell stories?"

"That's an extra." He smiled, the kind of smile Katie imagined the Pied Piper gave the kids before he led them out of Hamelin, playing his pipe and dancing. "We can film an episode and then you can send it out to the different stations. A long, tedious, frustrating process. But there's another way to get noticed."

Katie's stomach tightened and she fought an urge to

put her hands over her ears. She didn't know what he was going to say, but she was sure she didn't want to hear it.

It had better not involve wearing a swimsuit while doing her pie segment.

Or worse, no swimsuit. Their show would be *The Nude Cooks*. Rosa would have to watch out for grease splatter, while Katie would just get flour splotches.

"Tell us." Rosa crossed her arms, her voice heavy with suspicion.

Katie crossed her arms, too. There was too much change already, happening too fast, and she was pretty sure she wasn't a fast woman.

FIVE

L ooking at the two women with their crossed arms, Gabe thought, *Tough crowd*.

But he would win this.

His gaze lingered on the younger woman. She was...not ordinary, though she dressed ordinary, as if she tried to fit in. Not slouching but not standing tall, either.

The camera would show the truth of her. It would love the high cheekbones, the triangular chin, and the angles in her face. The sweetness, goodness and even a bit of edginess.

When she saw the film, he guessed she would be surprised and pleased—and a little shocked—to see herself as others saw her.

His gaze switched to Rosa. A classic Italian beauty with the kind of striking looks that didn't fade with age. As if she were a goddess who'd come down to earth for the span of a human life. He grinned. You could take the goddess out of Mount Olympus, but you couldn't take the goddess out of the woman.

He didn't allow himself to look below their necks. This was business. But when he'd entered the cottage kitchen, he'd given each woman a quick sweeping glance. He'd seen enough to know the pictures his uncle had sent didn't lie. They weren't deficient there. Not by any measure.

The viewers would eat them up.

"Well?" Rosa asked. In another moment she'd be tapping the toe of her shoe on the floor. Like a bull, she wanted to take charge. Maybe she didn't have balls, but for a long time Gabe had suspected a vagina was a hell of a lot stronger.

He held back a laugh. This was the wrong time to think of vaginas or testicles or any body parts. Food and money. That's what he needed to think about.

"A lot of chefs are trying to make it," he said. "On the Food Channel, the Travel Channel, the Top Chef shows, the morning shows, the afternoon shows, any show they can get. Most with impressive credentials and awards."

Rosa gave him a stare that reminded him of his fourth grade teacher when he displeased her. "I don't care." A faint southern Italian accent thickened her voice like honey sliding out of the hive. "I believe in myself."

"You'll need to believe in yourself. Your competition isn't coming from neighborhood diners. They're from four-star restaurants. Everyone wants to be famous."

She narrowed her eyes. "Are you trying to discourage us?"

He glanced at Katie. Her gaze was switching back and forth between him and Rosa, a frown puckering her forehead as she waited for them to duke it out.

"I'm telling you the truth," he said, turning back to Rosa.

"In that case, we don't need you." Rosa took a decisive step out the door.

He stayed planted on the cream-tiled kitchen floor. "There's another way to get in."

Rosa stopped. Her narrow-eyed stare could have bored holes in his brain. "I'm not sleeping with anyone."

He laughed so hard he had to wipe tears from his eyes. When he sobered, both women were frowning at him as if he were a turd on the sidewalk.

"What kind of mind do you have?" he asked.

"The kind of mind that knows how men think."

He grinned. This was turning out to be more fun than he'd hoped. "A friend—a *woman* friend—is a shoe addict. She started putting videos on YouTube that showed off her shoes. Telling viewers where she bought them and how much they cost, where she wore them, and what people said about them. The videos are fun and funny and short. Viewers have found her. She signed up for an advertising program. It's been a year. Her views are in the high six figure mark, and she's making good money."

"Advertisers?" Rosa's forehead furrowed. "On YouTube?"

"You know what YouTube is, don't you?"

"It's a place with videos of people doing silly things."

"Or singing songs," he said. "Or cute cats doing cute things. Or clips from weddings. And sometimes..." he let his voice croon... "cooking. The money you get for each view is small, but the more viewers, the more the money adds up."

The lines on her forehead deepened. She shifted her gaze to Katie. "What do you think?"

"It might be cheaper."

"It might be faster." Rosa's tone was considering, but she frowned even fiercer. Gabe could practically see her creating an Excel sheet in her head, pros on top, cons on the bottom.

It was his job to make the pro list longer. He needed to convince her that his vision was the better choice for her.

"You could build an audience with the shorter clips," he said, getting Rosa's attention and holding it. "All the money would go to you. Not to the TV station, which would give you a tiny percent. But to *you*." And to him. They'd each get their fair share. "I know a way to help with the costs."

"What's that?" Once again her eyes narrowed in suspicion. With eyes like that, she didn't need to talk.

His gaze traveled to Katie. Her lips were partly open. With her reddish brown hair, he'd expected brown or green eyes, but they were blue gray, reminding him of a rainy day sky. And something else. Something he couldn't quite grab hold of...

He frowned and looked back at Rosa. This was the wrong time to let his mind wander. He had an idea to sell. No, not an idea. A dream. Under his guidance, it could be a lucrative one for all three of them.

"I'll do it for one-third of the show. I'll produce it. I'll pay my own salary." He grinned at them, his heart pumping. He was fighting for this, and it had been a long time since he fought for anything. "And I'm *very* expensive."

"So are we," Rosa said, her tone militant.

"I can tell that by looking at you." He switched his gaze to Katie who was watching him as if he were an exotic snake. "And you." He heard his voice lower, a note in it that didn't belong in the kitchen. At least, not with Rosa watching.

He quickly turned back to Rosa to see her hands on her hips. Her lips twisted, mocking him, as if she saw the lust in his mind.

He grinned again. After all, he was a man. And he was lusty. And sometimes that led him into making mistakes. Mistakes like Cherise.

Some things just couldn't be turned off, even if they came up at the wrong place, wrong time and wrong woman.

And this was the wrong place, wrong time and Katie sure the hell was the wrong woman. Too diffident. He always went for the outgoing, decisive women. Not a woman who baked pies in her dead grandmother's cottage.

Rosa's derision changed to a scowl.

Already his libido was causing problems.

"We'll do the pilot," Rosa said. "I don't want to compromise until I've at least tried to sell my show."

He shrugged, the buoyancy sputtering out of him. "It's going to take a long time to shop it around. Do you even know who to send it to?"

Her chin went up. "My sons can find out."

"They have connections at the cable stations?"

"The local one."

"And what will the local cable station pay?"

Rosa's nostrils flared. "That will be between me and the station. Once I get on the station, we'll have more shows to shop around."

He raised his eyebrows slightly, shook his head slightly and lifted his shoulders slightly. Sending small signs of doubt without being too actively negative. If she settled for the local cable station, no way would it pay her enough to afford him. Not in an area where the biggest employer was a cheese factory.

But when a women talked to him in that tone, as if she was about to pour the nearest scalding cup of coffee on his head if he dared disagree, there was nothing else to do.

At least he'd be paid for the pilot. As he told her, he was expensive. He doubted she'd be able to afford a second time.

He'd been so sure this would be *it*—the project to pull him out of his slump, to bring back his mojo. He'd been wrong, but he didn't allow himself to feel regret. Coming here was still a good thing. Since Africa, he'd been skating through an empty life with a smile. His eyes wide open but not really seeing.

And then his uncle had sent him the picture and something about it had stunned him. Woken him. Made him want to jump back into life.

He'd thought this project was his fate, but apparently it was just his catalyst.

"You still want to start tomorrow?" Rosa asked.

"Tomorrow's good."

A sound came from Katie's throat, and he turned his attention to her.

"You okay?" he asked.

"Fine." Her voice was too high and too thin. "What time are you coming? I have pies to make and deliver in the morning."

"What time do you want us to start?" He kept his gaze on her face. Watching her wasn't hard to do. The hard part was holding back the charm. Because he wanted to charm her. Hell, he already wanted to do more. His mind knew she was wrong for him, but his body disagreed.

He'd just come out of a situation where he'd mixed business and pleasure. A mistake he didn't want to repeat. He was a man who loved life and women, and most of all he loved making them feel good. Feel *very* good. But this woman was hands off. At least until the pilot was completed.

"I usually finish delivering by seven in the morning," Katie said. "Later in the day, I prep for the next day." She made a face and pushed her hair back from her forehead. "I'm probably the last person who should do the show."

"Don't worry," Gabe said. "The camera will love you. My first thought when I saw you was that you're a natural." He lied. That had been his second thought. His first thought had been that he was going to enjoy this gig.

They talked about what they planned to do the next day. He wasn't surprised by Rosa's choice of meatball and home-made tomato sauce. "The basics of great Italian cooking," she said, then turned to Katie who had the mouse-trapped-by-a-cat look.

"Apple pie is a basic," Katie said. "Or pumpkin. I could do either."

"Katie's apple pies are the best I've eaten. So are her apple pies." Rosa sat straight, looking inward, her lips curving up, her actions telling Gabe more than her words.

"I use my gram's recipes," Katie said. "She got them from her grandmother."

"You'll share that," he said.

She nodded, still looking cautious, as if there were a snake in the room and it was him.

"It's just going to be me tomorrow." He softened his voice and smiled at her, playing the avuncular uncle instead of the Big Bad Wolf. "And Taz, my sound guy. No audience. Nothing to make you nervous."

"I'm not nervous." Her voice pitched even higher.

"You'll be fine." Rosa leaned toward Katie, her firm tone compelling Katie to be fine.

"I'm sure I will be." Katie gave a jerky nod, and Gabe silently moaned. Rosa wasn't helping. A firm hand wasn't needed here, just a light one.

But he wasn't telling Rosa that. This was a one-shot deal for him. He'd film the pilot for her, take the money, and then he was out of Miracle.

He'd thought the magic might be here, but he was wrong. His uncle had told him about Rosa's cheating husband, sounding a bit disgruntled that just as she was free of "the jerk" he was moving to Miami to join a his friend's fish business just as she'd be free.

Gabe would have to call him and tell him he'd made the right choice. Rosa's distrust of his gender was too new and too powerful right now for either of them to get what they wanted from her. In another few months she might listen to Gabe but by that time he'd have moved on.

If the miracle struck him again, it wouldn't be in the village of Miracle.

SIX

Taz, Gabe's sound guy, was like an exotic flower in Katie's kitchen, thin and tall with soulful, chocolate pudding eyes and skin the color of caramel. She guessed he was a couple years younger than her, and he kept shooting her flirtatious glances that made her stifle giggles and Rosa roll her eyes and then laugh. Gabe gave him the kind of look that Katie's dad had given Pastor Jerry ever since Katie's cousin Becky had caught him getting a blow job by one of his parishioners.

Katie imagined Wegner's was busy today, Linda Wegner's whispers hissing down the aisles of groceries and pharmacies and whatnots. She was probably in gossip heaven. Katie had only told her father about the filming, and he wasn't the gabby type. But Rosa most likely told her three sons, so Katie was pretty sure the news was out.

Amber, pregnant with Mike's baby, was probably using this as an excuse for her affair with Mike—even though that didn't make sense. But Katie had gone to school with Amber since they were six, and she could testify that *sense* and *Amber* didn't belong in the same sentence any more than non-fat whipped topping belonged in Katie's refrigerator.

Katie wished Trish were here to share the filming with her. The last time she'd talked to Trish was two weeks ago. Not hearing from her best friend was like a pinch in her heart.

She turned her attention back to the scene in front of her. The smell of tomatoes, basil and olive oil was making Katie's mouth water. If she let herself, she'd be drooling. That along with her drooping eyelids would look as attractive on TV as a dead rat. The viewers would think she was the village pie idiot. They could call her "the pie savant."

She leaned back on the kitchen chair and wished she were in her bed, softly snoring along with Happy the Beagle.

"That's it," Gabe said in his velvety voice, and Katie's breaths slowed as her spine curved into the chair, her head as light as her body was heavy. As if her brain floated inside a fluffy cloud.

"You mean you're done?" Rosa said.

"That's what I said." His voice had a laugh in it, and Katie smiled. That's why she liked him. Because he laughed silently at life.

She laughed at life a lot, but she did most of it when she was alone.

"Next time I'll say 'it's a wrap,'" Gabe said. "Will that make you feel better?"

"Very funny," Rosa said.

Katie's eyes closed, and she smiled again as she let the clouds in her mind take her away. Flying, she was flying. No worries about Rosa. No worries about Trish. What a wonderful feeling.

"Hey, wake up." A hand touched her shoulder, and she jerked her chin and her eyelids up. "Didn't you sleep well last night?"

Staring into Gabe's eyes, so close to hers, she felt herself drowning in his bright blue gaze. She started to raise her hand to his face, but it was too much effort. In her head, words formed. *Are you an angel?*

"How did you know?" she asked instead, the words slow and kind of slurred as she talked around her tongue that felt too big for her mouth.

The soft pad of his thumb brushed her cheek. He laughed softly. "Because you were sleeping. We're taking a break. Why don't you take a nap?"

Another thought drifted into her mind. *I'll take a nap with you.*

"Katie?" Rosa's voice colored with concern.

Katie blinked, the cloud disappeared and she thumped down to earth. Rosa stepped next to Gabe, a frown worrying her forehead.

"I'm awake." Katie straightened her spine. "I'm fine. I don't need a nap."

Gabe smiled, as if he'd read her thoughts. "Take all the time you need. I won't rush you."

Delicious. He was pure deliciousness.

"You're very comforting," she said. "I suppose you have a girlfriend or wife."

His smile deepened, the blue in his eyes shining brighter. "Not anymore."

A choked laugh came from Taz, and Katie stood, her face heating. She told them she'd be back in a moment then stepped over her snoring Beagle to hurry to the bathroom. Luckily her hair didn't need much more than a fluffing and her makeup was still intact. When her cheeks cooled, she took a deep breath and headed back to the kitchen.

She'd made up her mind.

He didn't have a girlfriend. He was planning to stick around for at least another day to make a rough edit for Rosa before leaving.

Why not take advantage of it? Why not have a fling? A one-night stand? He hadn't said anything to show he was attracted to her, but she'd noticed the way his gaze lingered on her, the heat in his eyes and the caress in his voice.

She didn't normally do flings, but why not now? He seemed...safe. And he for sure was seductive. The next day he would leave, and her life with her pies and her kitchen, with her dad and her friends nearby wouldn't change.

And she would have something wonderful to remember. The way people told her they remembered her pies. As if her pies made their lives happier.

That's how she imagined a night with him would make her feel, though she was probably delusional. He might turn out to be selfish in bed. More concerned with his own pleasure instead of hers.

In the kitchen again, Katie took out her pre-measured little bowls of ingredients and set them on the counter as Gabe checked the lighting, peering through a camera on a tripod. Taz angled a boom microphone over her head and asked her to speak for a sound check.

Setting a pumpkin on the counter, Katie said, "My father grows apples and pumpkins on his farm, so apple and pumpkin pies have been a staple on our farm every fall. This year, we've had a good—" Her mouth still open, she stepped back, her skin prickling, staring at the *thing* crawling up the cupboard.

"What is it?" Gabe asked. "You forget something?"

"A bug." She pointed. It wasn't just any bug. It was a big, juicy, hairy thing that looked as if it had crawled out of an evil scientist's lab.

Both men stayed with their equipment as Rosa hurried over to her.

"Whack it," Taz said.

Gabe watched her with a close-mouthed smile, waiting to see what she would do.

"It's a monster bug," Rosa said. "I've never seen one like that."

Still hanging back, Katie nodded. If she had to, she would take care of it. But she didn't want to get closer to it. It gave her the creeps.

"Which one of you is going to kill it?" Rosa gave them the same stare she gave her sons. The one that made them jump before she opened her mouth and said, "Jump."

"That's not in my job description," Taz said. "Just 'cause I'm a guy doesn't mean I have to kill bugs."

Rosa sniffed as if she smelled something bad. "Women need men for only two things. The second thing is killing bugs."

"If I don't kill the bug," Gabe said, "I forfeit my manliness?"

Rosa raised her eyebrows. "Your manliness is leaking out of you by the second, pretty boy."

Gabe laughed. "What's the first thing men are good for?"

Katie laughed and his gaze shifted to her. "If you have to ask..."

His gaze grew more intense. Katie wanted to look away but couldn't. As if she couldn't move until he released her.

"Are either of you going to kill this abomination?" Rosa snapped.

"Gabe, you do it," Taz said. "I'm better at the first thing."

A corner of his mouth kicking up, Gabe blinked. So did Katie, backing up a step, her legs wobbly. He left his camera on the tripod and headed around the counter where Katie handed him a paper towel. Bending forward, he nudged the bug onto the paper towel. Holding it as if it were a precious egg, he strode to the back hall. They heard the door clang and a second later, he returned with an empty paper towel.

Rosa and Katie clapped. Katie felt a grin stretch across her face. "My hero," Rosa said. Katie blew him a kiss. He laughed and turned to Taz who was watching with an *I'm too cool to kill a bug* sneer.

"Just for future reference," Gabe said, "a guy who won't do the second thing isn't going to be good at the first." Then he shifted his gaze to Katie, as if giving her the message that he was very good at the first thing.

Her legs felt weak again and she sucked in a gulp of air, unable to look away from him. Her breath stopped until he turned back to his camera. She exhaled shakily. Stepping up to the counter, she frantically tried to gather her brains and remember what she was supposed to do first.

Introduce herself. She'd forgotten to do that the last time. She needed to say her name without sounding like the village idiot.

Gabe and Taz weren't ready yet, so she mentally went over the steps to make the pumpkin pie, though she normally made the pie without even thinking about what she needed to do. It had been a long time since she looked at the recipe in her grandmother's faded handwriting with the round loops. But she looked now, and the memories grounded her, made her feel loved and cared for.

Her dad was great, but it was her grandmother who'd healed her when her mother dropped her off and said she couldn't do this anymore. Katie had a hard time remembering the first five years with her mother. Just scraps of memories of being scared and alone and often hungry. Her mother passed out. Sometimes there was a man snoring in her mother's bed. The next time there would be a different man.

And sometimes Katie dreamed she was a child and other children were making fun of her. Except for a boy with blond curls...

Like Gabe's hair, though his was wavy instead of curly.

"Ready?" Gabe asked Taz.

Taz leered at Katie. "I'm always ready."

"Be careful of this one," Rosa said, sitting at the table. "He's a player." She switched her attention to Gabe. "And be more careful of this one."

"In the heart." Gabe slapped his hand over his heart. "You're slaying me."

"I doubt that you'd die that easily," Rosa said.

"You're right. I don't die easily at all." He turned back to Katie. "Let's roll."

She was about to scratch her eyebrow but quickly brought down her hand. "Uh. I'm Katie Guthrie and I make pies." She smiled at the camera and guessed it looked like a scared grimace.

"Let's try that again," he said.

"Take in a few deep inhales and exhales before you talk," Taz said. "Relax. We all know Gabe's ugly, but try not to sound like you're talking to an IRS agent."

Katie laughed nervously. When they left, she would have a glass of wine, a piece of pie—maybe two pieces of pie—then curl up on her bed and sleep for an hour.

But first she had to get through this.

SEVEN

"You'll be wonderful," Gabe said. "Pretend you're talking to your lover."

"I don't think so." Katie heard the breathiness of her voice, like Marilyn Monroe singing *Happy Birthday, Mr. President.* Cringing inside, she continued, "I don't tell my lovers how to make a pie. I just bake pies for them."

His blue eyes seemed to glow, and her skin warmed. "A friend, then," he said. "Tell a friend."

She took in a breath and said her name. It felt odd. In the tiny village of Miracle, everyone knew her name.

The intro done without too much wobbling of her voice, she went through her talk once. Then went through it again. Then went through it seven more times, though Rosa only had to go through hers three times. Katie was ready to start again when Gabe said, "I think we've got it."

The tension seeped out of her. "Thank God."

Everyone laughed and Taz started to pull back the boom that angled over her head. Gabe put his hand out, stopping him. "Just one more thing. Tell us, why pies? Why not cakes or cookies or cupcakes?"

"You don't need this." Rosa's voice was sharp. "I'm making a cooking show, not an interview show."

He looked at her. "I won't charge more for this."

Rosa shrugged. Sitting back with her legs crossed, she

nodded at Katie to continue.

"Well..." Katie wrinkled her nose and switched from one foot to the other. Finally she leaned forward over the counter. "Pies are love."

He laughed softly. "Tell me how pies can be love."

"Not every pie."

"Your pies are?" His left eyebrow and a corner of his mouth quirked up.

He didn't believe her.

She stood straight. "I send love into the pies as I make them. I think of someone eating them, and for those few minutes I feel them with their eyes closed as they taste the deliciousness of the pie. At peace, all their troubles gone."

"That's a lot to ask of one piece of pie."

"Not for my pies." She heard the strength of conviction in her voice, talking directly to him. She knew the camera and sound were running, but it didn't matter. Rosa certainly wouldn't put this on her show. "Think of a two pie crust, like apple pie. The bottom crust is death and the top is birth. And in between, everything is happy. There's no sad in pies."

He grinned widely. "I've got to tell you, I've eaten some sad pies."

"Not *my* pies. Not if you do it right."

"Doing it right is important?"

"Of course. If you don't make a pie right, it won't taste good."

"What about life? Is it important doing that right?"

She shifted, feeling uncomfortable. "Why ask me that? This is supposed to be about pies."

"You said pies are like life. You compared the crusts to birth and death."

"Oh." Now it sounded stupid, and she was really glad

no one but the four of them would see this. "I guess it's important to do everything as well as you can. I have a wonderful life, with great friends and a wonderful father. But it's nothing I tried to do. I'm just lucky that way."

"And you make wonderful pies," he said.

She nodded. "Yes, I make wonderful pies. Is that all?"

Taz laughed and so did Rosa. Gabe nodded. "That's all."

Only then did she smile. Putting her palms on the counter, her fingers splayed, she leaned forward. "Wait until you eat my pie. Then you'll know."

"Can't wait," he said, the glow in his eyes making her skin warm. Then he bent to dismantle the camera. "I think it will look good."

Really? she wanted to ask. *Really, truly?* Like a child needing a pat on her back. Instead, she smiled stiffly and crossed to the cupboard at the end of the kitchen.

"I'll look at this on the computer in my room tonight," he continued. "I think it will be great."

She climbed on the step stool to pull a cardboard pie box out of the top cupboard. "You like pumpkin pie?" she asked, climbing down. "You can have it."

"Yes," Taz said.

"No, you don't," Gabe said. "Who carried the bug out of the house?"

"You can't eat the whole pie by yourself."

"You want to bet money on it?" Gabe put the camera in its bag, and he and Taz continued their bickering while she packed the pie along with paper plates, plastic forks and a plastic knife.

Rosa took her sauce and meatballs out of the fridge, saying it was dinner for her youngest son tonight so she wasn't leaving them any. Her features were pulled tight, and she spoke faster than usual instead of dwelling on the words. No doubt thinking of her second oldest son who still worked at Fabrini's with his dad and her oldest at a culinary college in New York.

Carrying the pie to Gabe, Katie frowned, her steps slow, as if she carried fifty pounds of sorrow instead of one of the best tasting pumpkin pies in the world.

Why did some men have to be assholes? What was wrong with them? If she were a man, she would be happy to have a wife like Rosa.

When Rosa walked by a group of men, their heads turned. Besides that, she was smart and she could cook.

How could Mike want Amber more than her?

She scowled at Gabe as he zipped his tripod in a case. "Here." She thrust the pie at him along with a container of whipped cream. "You take it."

His gaze sympathetic, as if he knew what she was thinking, Gabe slung the tripod and the camera over his shoulders. Only then did he take the pie and the whipped cream. "You were great," he said.

"I am great." She held her head high, and expected him to smile again, but he just looked at her eyes and her mouth, saying nothing.

"You doing anything tonight?" Taz asked.

Aware of Gabe's gaze on her, she shook her head. "I'll be doing prep work for tomorrow. Sorry."

Taz shrugged. "Good luck on selling the pilot." From his lack of enthusiasm, she guessed he thought there wasn't a chance of a key lime pie in hell.

A snort came from the table in the corner of the kitchen. The sound of an old Beagle awakening. Then claws tapped on the floor, Happy limping toward her, though with the cataracts that made her eyes look glassy, Katie guessed she only saw her silhouette. Or maybe Happy smelled her. Happy's nose still seemed to work, as well as her appetite and her ability to love.

Both men said their goodbyes then headed out to the back door, Taz first. Seconds later the storm door clanged shut and the butterflies in Katie's chest stopped twirling, as if they all dropped down dead with disappointment.

Why did Taz have to ask her out instead of Gabe? She shouldn't have made up an excuse. She should have just smiled, thanked him and said no. No explanation needed.

Then Gabe might have asked her out.

Or not. While she'd been thinking of a fling, he'd probably been eager to leave.

Huffing breaths reminded her that she had responsibilities. "Come on, sweetie." She scooched down with her hands out to Happy whose head was bobbing up and down, tongue out.

Love for her valiant dog filled Katie. A large-capacity refrigerator full of love, she thought as she lifted Happy, then nuzzled her nose on Happy's ear.

"Love you," she whispered, though Happy didn't hear anything she said unless she yelled. Bringing her head up, Katie saw Gabe in the doorway. Staring at her.

Her breath stopped and she couldn't breathe.

Then he nodded and left. Gone.

EIGHT

Pumpkin pie reminded Gabe of his childhood in fall: raking leaves, carving pumpkins, Thanksgiving turkey dinner with his mom, stepfather and two half-sisters, a phone call from his dad in California with his new wife. In his motel room, Gabe added one more person to that list.

Katie Guthrie. Shy, sly and sexy. She spoke softly and baked a mean pie.

He sat behind the desk in the corner and watched the video of Rosa first. Not cutting anything yet, just watching with an editing eye. Taz swaggered in as it was wrapping up.

"You better've saved a piece of pie for me," he said.

Gabe stopped the video. "Or what? You'll never work for me again?"

"Or I'll punk you big time."

"You would, too." Gabe slid the pie across the desktop toward him. Taz had a twisted mind, and Gabe wasn't in the mood for practical jokes. What he was in the mood for was one tall woman with great cheekbones and eyes the color of a foggy sky...but that wasn't going to happen.

Taz scooped out a piece then topped it off with more than his share of whipped cream. Only then did he sit and take a bite, his eyelids lowering. "Umm, there really is something special about this pie. I'm feeling the love."

"Yeah, I'm a believer." Gabe looked at the pie,

wanting more, but since he'd already eaten two pieces, he decided to wait until later for the third.

"I'm thinking of eating Mexican tonight," Taz said, his mouth full. "The one we saw on the main drag."

Gabe doubted there were any drag races in the city of Tomahawk, a smallish city with aging buildings about a twenty minute drive from Miracle. With a coat of new snow, colored lights on store windows and wreaths on lampposts, the main street wouldn't look out of place on a Christmas card.

"I'll pass. I want to watch the tape."

"Eager to get back to your woman in Chicago?"

"Cherise isn't my woman anymore."

"For sure? I gotta say, she was uppity."

"Uppity?" Gabe laughed again, and he realized in this one day he'd laughed more than in the last month with Cherise.

He didn't blame her. He blamed himself and the funk attached to him like a second, unwanted skin.

"She's one of those black hole joy suckers," Taz said. "Spend too much time with them and they suck the joy outta you."

Gabe shrugged. "Before we moved in together, she was different."

Taz nodded like an old man who'd seen it all instead of a young dude in his prime. "Women do that. Most of 'em, anyway. Some asshole guys, too. My sister's ex was like that. Once joy suckers like that get in your bed and your space, they think they got you like this." He held out his hand, palm up, then curled his fingers into a fist. "You may as well slit your throat, 'cause you're no better than road kill." He nodded again, his lower lip overlapping the top. Another old man move. "Smart thing not to marry Cherise."

"Survival instincts. She's part of my history now."

"And you learn from history?"

"What are you?" Gabe narrowed his eyes at Taz. "My mom?"

"Wrong gender, dude. If you're not coming with me, you going back to Katie?"

"She said she was busy."

"She shot me down, but I could tell she wanted you. And you wanted her." Taz jabbed his plastic fork at Gabe. "The air stank of sex."

"Yet you asked her out."

Taz shrugged. "Never know for sure until you give it a try. If you don't want her, maybe I'll try again. If you're not going back, she might change her mind."

Gabe stared at him. Not saying anything, just staring. Keeping his body relaxed. His face calm. But not taking his eyes off his friend with the younger body and the beautiful caramel-skinned face that made women melt like butter in the sun.

Taz laughed. "I get the hint. She's all yours."

"I never said that."

"Yeah, sure." Taz gestured at the computer. "Did you watch them?"

"Just Rosa. She looks great on film."

"No brainer there. What about Katie? She's the make-or-break one."

"Aren't you going out to eat?"

"No rush." Taz got up and dragged the chair closer to the desk. "Turn it around so I can see. Give it a go."

Gabe shrugged. No reason not to. But something inside him itched. He wanted to watch the film of Katie alone, not with Taz making comments. Ignoring the itch, Gabe angled the computer so they could both see.

Katie appeared for her sound test, something he

normally didn't waste film on. He didn't know why he did this time, but he instantly felt electrified. As if struck by lightning as he watched her on his laptop screen. He'd been right about the camera loving her. Loving her face, her red-brown hair, her height. She wore a green apron, but even with the apron, the viewer could tell Katie's breasts were not defective.

Film wasn't about looks, though. Not even close. It was about personality; like Oprah, Ellen, Rachel Ray. All of them outgoing and, in Rachel Ray's case, perky. The last word Gabe would use to describe Katie would be perky.

She started to talk in a kind of robotic way. A no-no. But then she jumped back, seeing the bug, and Rosa came into the scene. Taz laughed and so did Gabe. It was a good bit. Though Rosa did most of the talking, Gabe's gaze kept travelling to Katie. Watching the expressions flash across her expressive face, all her walls down.

"Perfect," Taz said.

Gabe shrugged. No one was perfect. Taz would know that in a few years. But who wanted perfect? That would bore him.

"It's good," he said.

"You're not bad, either." Taz grinned at him.

"I like being behind the camera. Now, shut up and watch."

Rosa went back to the table, and Katie started again, flubbing her intro, the first syllable out of her mouth the dreaded *uh*. Gabe heard himself telling her to make her voice looser, and she spoke in a breathy voice, saying she didn't tell her lovers how to make a pie.

His body tightened.

Jesus, she was good.

She started again without the *uh*. Not great, not bad.

Not a ball of fire like Rachel Ray, but it didn't matter, he couldn't take his eyes off her.

It wasn't a surprise. Just looking at the picture his uncle sent him had made his heart beat faster. But he'd promised himself he wouldn't mix business with pleasure again as he did with Cherise. A bad idea, making those kind of promises. He was like a kid spotting a ball in the grouchy neighbor's yard. Knowing he wasn't supposed to play with it, but unable to stop himself.

That kid had been him.

As a kid, the more untouchable it was, the more he wanted to touch.

He'd thought he'd gotten over it.

Shutting off his thoughts, he paid attention to the video. Katie relaxed a bit more the next take. Then again. And again. And again. In her quiet way, she commanded his attention. Not just his, either. Taz slid to the edge of his seat, his head inches from Gabe's so he could see the screen better.

And then the cooking scene ended, and anticipation built inside Gabe.

This was what he'd been waiting for. He heard his own voice asking "...why pies?"

His breath sucked in.

"Pies are love," she said...and the look on her face, as if she were transcendent, made his heart thunder.

He gripped the wood chair arms and watched her, transfixed. Not able to take his gaze from the screen.

When it was over, he sat back, dazed. He slowly turned to look at Taz. Wondering if the younger, cooler friend looked as stunned as he did.

"You might have a winner," Taz said, grinning. Not dazed but seeing the screen magic.

"Not me. Them." Gabe jerked his head at the laptop, as if tiny people lived inside it instead of tiny pixels. Rosa had hired him to make the video. That was all. She'd planned from the beginning to shop it around herself. Not a good idea, but he saw her point. Who cared more about her success?

"Rosa might sell this after all," he said. "The two of them...they're special."

"Could be. But I bet they aren't the only hot chick duo with no credentials shopping their show around." Taz stood. "That last bit with Katie, that was different. That was hot."

Gabe didn't answer. Staring at the frozen image of Katie on the laptop monitor, relief on her face that the filming was over.

In his mind, an idea bubbled up.

He pushed up from the chair then lowered back into it. Katie had said she'd be busy. If she got up so early in the morning, she might be in bed now. This could wait until late tomorrow morning.

Much better to see her when she was wide awake with her brain fully functioning before talking her into changing her life.

NINE

"I want you to see something." The intensity in Gabe's eyes made Katie's breath hitch. "Something that could change your life."

Katie blinked at him. This was the second morning she had an angel in her kitchen, though she suspected he had the devil in him. An angel wouldn't make her skin warm from the inside out and her fingertips tingle.

"It's very odd." She eyed the laptop he was holding.

His smile bloomed. So did a wave of heat and confusion inside her, but she kept her attention on his face.

"What's odd?" he asked.

"It's odd that every time the doorbell rings lately, it's someone who wants to change my life. I'm only doing this cooking show thing to help Rosa. I like my life as it is." Her hands curled as she looked up at him. She half expected him to use his charm on her.

Instead he went still, as if he were processing what she said. As if he really listened to her.

"Who said I wanted to change your life?"

She shook her head, unable to answer, but her skin prickled. This man was about to jerk her out of her comfortable life. She didn't know why, but she was as sure of it as she was sure Happy loved her from the tip of her moist nose to the end of her waving tail.

"I don't want you to do anything you don't want to,"

he said, finally breaking the silence.

A laugh and a cry struggled inside her. He was good at this. As if he knew her mind and emotions the way she knew pies.

And she...right now she felt like uncooked pie dough. "Okay, I'll listen to you."

He nodded, as if this was serious stuff. "I'll listen to you, too."

If this were the Victorian age, she thought, she might swoon. But she was no Victorian lady wearing swoon-inducing stays, though he was certainly swoon-worthy. "Would you like anything to drink?" She stepped back and hit the counter with her butt. "Coffee or tea? Pie?"

"Pie," he said, no hesitation. "Pumpkin?"

She laughed and heard the breathlessness in it again. She really needed to stop that. If she kept this up, she might as well lie on the kitchen table and say, "*Take me now*."

"You finished the pie already?"

"Not alone. Taz helped me. To keep him from eating my half, I had to threaten to break his fingers."

She stepped away from the counter, grateful to find her legs were steady. He loved her pie. Of course, everyone did, but his appreciation seemed to mean more. "Today's pie is banana cream."

His face lit up. "My favorite."

She crossed to the fridge, not surprised. Just as she hadn't been surprised to see him when she opened the back door. This morning when she'd been making pies for her deliveries, she'd had a sudden urge to make a banana cream pie. She'd known then that it was for Gabe. She'd known he was going to come to her house and eat a piece.

"Tea or coffee?" she asked. She couldn't tell him any

of that. He'd think she was crazy.

Gabe opted for coffee. A moment later they sat at the table, digging into their pies at the same time. He ate his first bite slowly, eyes half closed, as if it were a sensory experience.

She melted. Wanting to lean forward and kiss his face, his neck...wanting to sit on his lap and feed him bites of pie between kisses. She'd never seen anything sexier than the way he looked eating her pie, as if it were the food of Gods.

"You made this from scratch, didn't you?" he asked.

She nodded. "Always. I like the real thing."

He stilled, his expression intense for a second, his eyes brilliant. "When you do your own show, that's what you should call it, 'The Real Thing.'"

"Isn't that taken?" As soon as she said it, she realized she should have denied any intention of doing her own show.

"I'll check to see if we can use it."

"We? There is no *we*. And I don't plan on having my own show. For one thing, I promised to be on Rosa's show."

"First she has to sell it."

"If anyone can do it, she can."

He took another bite of her pie. She watched the bliss cross his face again, and she took another forkful of hers. She closed her eyes, tasting the blend of vanilla, banana, cream and sugar. Like a bite of heaven inside her mouth. Nothing mattered except for the perfect flavors. Nothing.

Then she opened her eyes and saw that everything mattered.

"How about 'Pie Me to the Moon'?" she asked.

He laughed. "Why not 'Katie's Pies'?"

She grimaced. He'd poked a sore spot. "Someone has

that name. I had to call my pie business 'Katie's Miracle Pies.'"

"I like that." His smile was back, his gaze saying he liked a lot of things about her.

She turned back to her pie. Now she was getting fanciful, imagining things in his gaze, though her life was fanciful every day. How many people had pies that talked to them? Whispering to her, telling her to make them?

He finished his pie first, but she finished shortly after. Happy looked up at her expectantly. Happy had a long memory back to when she first came as a puppy. Katie was young, too, and not as strict then. But now she had to think about Happy's health. As much as she hated to deny Happy, she did.

Most of the time. A little crust couldn't hurt.

She got up and scraped crumbs into Happy's food bowl in the corner. Happy barely waited for Katie to step away before she lunged forward and started licking.

When Katie turned to pick up Gabe's clean plate, he was watching her with an indulgent smile. The kind that most people used watching children do something cute.

Not the reaction she wanted from him.

"She's nineteen." Katie heard the defensive note in her voice. "And she loves my pies."

"That's ancient for a dog. Maybe your pies are magic."

Katie felt her eyes widen, but she walked forward because it was silly to think that...and she couldn't admit to him how often she believed it was true.

"Do you need a warm up?" She gestured to his mug.

"I'm good." He set his laptop on the table and opened it. "We need to do this."

"Actually, we don't need to do anything."

He attached a USB cord to the computer and the other end to the outlet two feet from the table before raising his head. "People are going to love you."

"People already love me." Her dad, she thought. And Happy. Though Happy wasn't exactly people, she mattered. So did her dad's dog, Tuck. Katie was Number Two in Tuck's doggy heart that was technically veins and arteries and muscle, but in reality was 100% love.

The barn cats had affection for her because she often changed their water and fed them, and she petted all the cats that came up to her.

Her mother sent her a birthday card every year and signed it Love, Raelyn.

Rosa loved Katie as a friend. Perhaps a few other women had *friend love* for her, though her best friend wasn't answering her calls anymore, and she didn't know why.

Three men had professed love to her, but none recently. It had been awhile since she'd had a desire to date. She knew every single guy in town and quite a few in the neighboring communities. Lately she'd begun to wonder whether she was asexual.

Until now.

"More people will love you," Gabe said. "People you don't even know." The laptop on the table lit up.

"Until another show comes along," she shot back.

His eyebrow arched. "You're tougher than you look."

"And proud of it."

He laughed softly. "You should be proud of this. Just a minute, I'll bring it up."

As she waited, she gazed at his profile and his lingering half smile. He was a smiler, with dimples in his cheeks and tiny crinkles that fanned out from the corners of his eyes. She liked that. Liked too many things about him.

He was her pie, she thought. Why him, she didn't

know. From the first time she saw him, it was like puzzle pieces clicking together.

But the problem with puzzle pieces was they had to fit in with all the other pieces to make the whole picture. And she didn't see how that was going to happen.

"Here." He angled the laptop so she could see the screen then scooted his chair next to hers, close enough for her to smell him. She breathed his scent in. Like nutmeg...only nothing like nutmeg.

A shiver went through her, and she leaned toward the laptop and saw her image on the screen, wearing a green apron and staring back at her. Her eyes were wide and her smile looked like a frightened grimace. Then she started to recite the script she'd clearly memorized, her voice and body language stiff, as if she were in fifth grade again, reading a poem in front of class.

Gabe bent over the keyboard. Mumbling that he didn't want to show the cooking part, he fast-forwarded to the end of the show. The video moved again at regular speed. She stood behind the counter but he was the one talking on the video, asking, "Tell us, why pies? Why not cakes or cookies or cupcakes?"

He must have edited Rosa's objections out, because she was wrinkling her nose then leaning over the counter and saying, "Pies are love."

His on-screen voice laughed softly. "Tell me how pies can be love."

Sitting next to her tormentor as she watched the screen, Katie groaned and laughed and covered her eyes and then uncovered them. Finally, the video ended, freezing with her bemused face looking back at her.

"What do you think?" he asked.

"I don't know." She couldn't think, as if banana cream pie filling was clogging up her brain cells.

He twisted in the chair, so close she could see three shades of blue in his eyes. See that his eyelashes were golden brown, darker than his hair. Close enough that she could lean forward and kiss him.

She drew in her breath.

"I thought it was great," he said. "So did Taz. Viewers will love it."

"You mean..." She sat back in her chair and shook her head. Shaking the thought of kissing him right out of her mind.

"I can't promise it will go viral, but I can promise a lot of views. Not with just this one—we'd have to do a series of similar videos to build your viewers. We can do it. You're passionate about pies. People love passion. They can get recipes anywhere, but what you have is unique. They'll love you. They'll want to watch you. They'll tell their friends about you."

She shook her head again. Sometimes she thought she might be a little insane, but she was nowhere near as insane as this man.

"I can't."

"You don't have to do anything. Leave it to me. I'll do it."

She shifted her gaze. Not toward the camera but toward the back door. Wishing she could step outside. The sun was out. Coming home this morning after delivering pies to the truck stop and the Italian restaurant in Tomahawk, she noticed a few yellow and orange leaves on the sugar maple tree in the front yard. In the dawn redness it looked like an old painting. She had an urge to go outside and see them now, in full sunlight.

"You're afraid," he said.

Her head snapped around. "No."

His eyebrows lifted. "It's very common. Some people are afraid of greatness."

"I bake pies." Her tone was sharp. What didn't this man understand about baking a pie? Anyone could do it. In fact, everyone *should* do it. If all the leaders of all the countries in the world went into their kitchens and made at least one pie every day, the world would no doubt be a better place.

Slowly, her breaths shallow, she turned her gaze back to him. He watched her. Unmoving. Implacable.

She wanted to kick him.

"I promised Rosa to do this with her. I can't do it with you."

"It's not the same thing. She's doing a show. What we're doing is small moments of time."

"You sound like a politician."

He put his hand over his heart. "You wound me."

"If the knife fits..."

Dropping his hand, he leaned closer again. Inches away. His blue eyes brilliant, enthralling her so she couldn't pull back or look away. "Think of the videos like movie trailers. If they become popular, it will make her show all the more valuable. In fact, I'll ask her to do some."

"She said yesterday she doesn't want to do short videos."

"Then she doesn't have to. It will be just you and me."

"You're worse than a bulldog."

"I promise..." his smile returned... "I don't bite."

She gritted her teeth and put both hands to her hair, grabbing handfuls. *This man. This insane man. Can't he leave me in peace?*

"You have no excuses," he said.

"I don't need an excuse. I don't want to do it."

"Because you're afraid. You have this...magic."

"Magic!" She stared at him. Her? She was the quiet one. Her pies were special, she didn't deny that. But she had nothing to do with it. It was a gift, the way another woman was born with a beautiful singing voice. The way Gabe was born to captivate her. "This is too much."

Emotion churned up inside her and she drew back from him. Her body started to shake, as if she were in the middle of an earthquake.

"Out." Her voice quaking, she pushed up from the chair. She was overreacting, she knew it, but right now she didn't care. "I just want you to leave. You didn't have to say that."

"You don't believe me." He shook his head, staying in his chair. "You really don't know how powerful you are."

"If I were powerful, you'd be a pile of ashes."

"Powerful doesn't mean the person who talks the loudest or laughs the loudest or has the most money." His gaze locked with hers, and she couldn't look away. "You're powerful because you care, and that shines out of you. You care about your dog, your friend, your grandmother. I know you cared for her. Love is powerful."

"You are..." She flailed her arms up. "Insane. Totally and horribly insane."

"Then humor an insane man." He smiled and once again his eyes glowed and she could practically feel him sending her waves of seduction that melted her muscles. "Do this for me. We'll try it a few times. It will prove who's right. You or me."

She plopped back down onto the chair. "I don't have to prove anything."

"Why does it scare you so much? You saw the bit." He gestured at the screen. "Once you relax, you're a natural.

Even if I'm prejudiced because I want to sleep with you, there's no failure in this. No risk. People either watch you or they don't. If they do and we get ads, we'll make money. If they don't…" He shrugged. "The only one who will lose money will be me."

She sat stunned. She heard everything he said, but the only thing that stuck in her head was that he wanted to sleep with her. A squeaking sound came out of her mouth, but she couldn't form words. Her brain seemed to have turned into pureed pumpkin.

"I believe in you." His voice was even and calm. He kept staring straight into her eyes, compelling her to go along with him. "What I want to know is, do you believe in yourself?"

As if his expression unfroze her voice, words spewed out of her mouth in a hot rush. "Yes. Yes, I do. Yes, I believe in myself."

He grinned and sat back. His intense gaze lessening, as if he were releasing her from a compulsion spell. Which was more crazy thinking. The result of reading the whole Harry Potter series. Real people didn't have compulsion spells. As for her magic pies… Some people could write songs by the time they were three. Others could do college math in third grade. She made pies.

Yes, they were magic, but everyone had magic. It's just that not everyone knew it.

"You know I meant…" She stopped, suddenly fighting laughter. "If Rosa gives her okay, I'll do it."

"Done." He slapped his hand on the table, as if he were sealing a deal. And he smiled at her like a man who'd just won the poker hand.

She guessed that made her the loser.

Slowly, she stood. This was the craziest day she could remember since she came to Miracle. This man was turning her calm and ordered life upside down.

"Do you have a card?" she asked. As if this were a normal conversation about business. As if he weren't crazier than her. Locked up, medicated and throw-away-the-key crazy. "I'll call you."

"Am I scaring you?" he asked. "Am I moving too fast?"

"Of course not."

"Then you won't mind if I do this." He stepped toward her, put his arm around her...and then he leaned so close to her she felt his breath on her skin. He pulled her against him and she closed her eyes and sighed, her body curving against his.

TEN

Her kiss was as luscious as her pie.

Gabe's brain was weakening, all the strength going to his penis. The head with no brain. He meant to do a quick kiss, but that was when his brain was running on full power. Now only a few cells fired inside it, screaming at him to pull back, to take it slow. That he was moving too fast with her.

But his body wanted her. Right now. With a need he hadn't felt...ever. As if something in the pie inflamed him. He'd never heard of a banana pie aphrodisiac, but something was happening to him. He wanted to take her on the table. Or the floor. Or carry her to her bedroom. Make love to her on a soft surface instead of a hard one. Kiss her neck. Her bare shoulders. Her breasts.

A snuffling sound came from behind him, but he ignored it. Jesus, he wanted to hold her breasts in his hands. And then lower. Slide his hands down her ribcage. Reach her belly. Stop and kneel and kiss it. Feel the warmth of her. The softness. Knowing that below his mouth on her skin was her womb.

And then lower, the heat and the woman smell drawing him like honey draws a bee.

The snuffling sound came again, a pig-like grunt.

"Stop." With a hoarse whisper, Katie put two hands on his chest, her fingers splayed, and shoved him off her.

He stepped back, her hands falling off his shoulders.

He felt dazed, as if he'd been hit by a bat. The blood still hadn't returned to his brain. She was staring at him with her lips parted, looking dazed, too. As though wondering what the hell happened.

That kiss was like a flower turning into a garden in a snap of time.

Another snuffle came and she looked down at Happy. "Come on, sweetie." Turning toward the back door, Katie lurched forward. She caught herself then walked steadily as he watched the way her ass swayed in her navy slacks. Like a metronome. Swinging back and forth, back and forth.

She could walk like that in front of him all the time. He could make a video of her walking, filmed entirely from the backside. Her ass could hypnotize him, the cheeks nicely padded, the hips wide. Good for child-bearing.

He slapped his hand to his forehead, knowing that wasn't his mind speaking. That was his primal instinct that wanted to populate the world with his seed. His mom used to say they had Viking blood in his family. For the first time he believed her.

His non-primal self didn't want to populate anything. It wanted to enjoy himself. To laugh. To eat good food—including pies. Lots of pies. And make his films. Show people as they were, with all their faults and all their greatness. Make them laugh and cry. Most of all, make them *feel*.

But right now he was the one feeling. An overload of emotions, all telling him to do the wrong thing that somehow felt so right.

The back door opened and cool air puffed into the kitchen. He needed colder air than that, but it would have to do. She said something to the dog who probably didn't hear her though her husky voice floated into the kitchen.

The need lessened slightly, the blood flowing upward, more brain cells firing, telling him it was a good thing the dog had interrupted them. That it wasn't a good idea to make love with her.

Yeah. Like he believed that.

Unplugging the USB cord, he heard a man's voice. Gabe stopped. Not even breathing. As if listening for a rival.

He shook his head at the thought. He wasn't a man staking his claim, watching out for rivals. Viking ancestors or not, he was just a man who wanted to make his videos. And maybe have a little fun. What man didn't want that?

But that kiss... He hadn't expected anything that intense. It was like starting a fire in a grill and having it flare up in his face.

As he shut down his laptop, he heard hard-soled boots hit the hall floor, and they didn't come from Katie. His muscles clenched, but he turned his head toward the back door and set his easy smile on charm, the way he did for the brides and grooms and their families who didn't seem to notice the emptiness in his eyes.

A tall, lean man with long, white-streaked black hair entered the kitchen, Katie and Happy behind him. His thin face had seen a lot of life and his eyes bored into Gabe. Though he wore a flannel shirt and jeans, Gabe easily pictured him as an outlaw in an old western. The kind of cowboy that drank hard, played hard and shot hard.

"Gabe, this is my father, Sam Guthrie. Daddy, this is Gabe Robbins." Katie's voice was breathy and her face was flushed. Softened. Like someone who'd just been kissed very thoroughly.

Gabe suspected he had the signs of arousal on his face, too, as desire still thrummed through his veins, like the last note on a guitar singing in the air. Hard to look a man in the face when two minutes ago you'd thought about taking his daughter on the table, the floor, against the wall. A man in such a primitive arousal that any surface would do.

It wasn't the first time Gabe had to talk himself out of an awkward situation. Taking a deep breath, he strode toward Katie's father, his hand out. Gabe made the instant decision to call him by his first name. Man to man, instead of one man to another man whose daughter he wanted to bang.

Sam looked at Gabe's hand then into his eyes for a long moment. Gabe was about to put his hand down when Sam took it. Not a handshake, just grabbing it and taking it.

Something happened to Gabe. For one second, two seconds, he froze while Sam's eyes pierced his as if trying to see inside his soul.

Then Sam released his hand, and Gabe's mind whirled. He started to wobble, and a slender hand gripped his arm.

"Daddy, you didn't!" Katie grabbed him and held him upright.

"I don't know what you're talking about, baby girl."

"You're impossible. Come on, help me get him into a chair."

Sam gripped Gabe's left arm. The father-daughter team half dragged, half pulled him to the kitchen table, then dumped him onto the chair he'd been sitting in when this all started. Gabe slumped back and looked up at the two faces staring down at him. One with a worried frown, the other with a curled lip.

"Did you just give me a Vulcan mind meld?"

"Daddy." Katie shook her head at her father, her lips flattened into a thin line.

"I don't know what you're talking about." Sam Guthrie's voice reminded Sam of a car driving over gravel, his dark eyes sharp like a vulture's. "I don't have pointy ears, and this isn't a *Star Trek* episode. You really think any of that is real?"

"Of course not," he said, though a smile played on Sam's mouth, and Gabe suspected there was more to the story. Something had happened. Something weird. It wasn't his imagination.

"Maybe you're not feeling well." Katie's gaze didn't quite meet his.

"Maybe it's a guilty conscience," Sam said.

"Daddy!" She glowered at her father. "What did you come here for, anyway?"

"Pie, sweetie." The muscles of his face relaxed and he looked slightly less intimidating. "And to say hi to my favorite girl."

"You don't need to sweet talk me for a piece of pie." She hurried to the counter. "I made banana cream."

Gabe watched her load a piece of pie on a plate. It seemed surreal. He felt like Alice in Wonderland with a sex change. But there were no magic mushrooms in sight. Just pie. The best damn pie he'd eaten.

Just thinking about it, energy whispered back into his body. He sat straighter. Not fully at speed but faking it. Sometimes he thought he was almost as good at faking small moments like these as a woman faking an orgasm.

Not that fakery ever happened in his bed.

"Thinking of something funny?" Sam set his pie plate on the table then took a chair. "Want to share that thought?"

"I'm not thinking of anything," Gabe said.

Sam narrowed his eyes at him. "I know what you're thinking when you say you aren't thinking."

Gabe's face warmed, and he knew his cheeks were turning red. The curse of being a blond. Lucky for him, women liked his blush and his wavy hair. Unlucky for him that their fathers never appreciated him as much. Sometimes the mothers didn't either. Other times they appreciated it a little too well.

"You should know my daughter tells me everything," Sam said.

"Dad! You liar."

Sam's shoulders heaved but he gazed at Katie with a straight face. "You mean you lie to me?"

"I mean I'm twenty-eight years old and some things are none of your business." She pointed her index finger at him. "Just like some of the things that go on in your house are none of my business."

His right eyebrow lifted. "You wound me, baby girl. It's a good thing you're a great baker." He dug his fork into his piece of pie. "Just like I taught you."

She rolled her eyes. "You're such a bullshitter." She turned to Gabe. "Would you like another piece?"

He sat straighter, his mind spinning, working again. "Yes," he said. The pie really didn't have any sex magic in it. That kind of thinking was crazy. Besides, it was always good to mirror what the person in power did. Katie seemed to be independent, though she lived in a cottage on her father's farm, but even with whipped cream coating his upper lip, Sam Guthrie gave off an air of being a man born with a natural power. One so sure and true he didn't have to do anything to impress people.

"So you're a farmer," Gabe said as Katie slid a piece of

pie onto a plate. "Do you have cows or chickens?"

He looked at Katie and saw her wince.

"We had chickens," Sam said, "but they were killed."

Katie shuddered. "A coyote, we think. Or a fox. My father just raises crops now."

"What kind of crops?" Gabe asked.

A look passed between father and daughter, the kind of look that meant secrets. Gabe wondered—

"Corn, wheat, that kind of stuff," Katie said as she put the plate with the piece of pie in front of him.

He picked up his fork. Later he could wonder. Right now was all about the pie.

ELEVEN

Gabe left, and Katie felt glad and sad at the same time. If Sam weren't here, she'd run into the living room and watch him drive away, like a lovesick teenager.

"So that's the guy," Sam said.

"The director, yes." She put the remaining pie in the fridge.

"There's something going on between the two of you."

"He wants to put the video he took of me on YouTube." She turned to him, the door slowly swinging shut. "He thinks people will like it, and it might even help Rosa sell her show."

Sam leaned back in his chair. "You're dressed?"

"Dad! I even have an apron on."

"You say anything embarrassing?"

She shook her head, though she found the whole process embarrassing. She was used to the attention being on her pies, not on her.

"Then do it."

"I told him already if it's okay with Rosa, it's okay with me."

"That's not the only thing going on with you."

"I'm twenty-eight." She gave him a warning look and wished she'd learned how to copy Rosa's stare. If Rosa could patent and sell it, she'd be an instant millionaire. "Anything going on is my business."

"Doesn't matter how old you are. You're still my baby girl."

She laughed, a fullness in her throat because she was lucky to be so loved and to love back. It had been a long time ago, but she remembered the feeling of not being loved. She remembered days and nights of bleakness and emptiness. She remembered enough that now she treasured her father and her friends.

Happy shuffled, waking up again in her corner. Making the slow, laborious process of pushing her body up until she stood on her short, arthritic legs.

The fullness in Katie's throat grew. She bent, scooped up Happy and carried her outside. Happy had just been out a short time ago, but this last year she'd been having accidents and it was better not to take chances.

She set down the Beagle so she could do what she had to do, knowing Happy wouldn't stay out long. When Happy was a young dog, she was a runner. Chasing rabbits, squirrels, birds and, on a few unfortunate occasions, skunks. Often staying away for a couple of hours until Katie had to search for her, her pocket full of treats to lure Happy home.

She used to get so angry at Happy.

Now she wished those days were back.

Leaving Happy outside to stare around and try to see through her cataract-covered eyes, Katie returned to the kitchen and hefted a big sigh.

"Something's wrong," Sam said, his eyes hard. "You sure it's not Gabe?"

"Forget him. Nothing's going on there."

He raised his eyebrows, and she shrugged. "A kiss, that's all. Just a kiss."

She grabbed the plates and the forks to put them in the dishwasher.

When she turned around, Sam still watched her with his eyes half lidded, as if he had all day and wasn't leaving until he found out what was bothering her. When she was young, she thought her father saw all and knew all. There was comfort in it. Not so much when she was a teen. And now...

Something broke in her. A ball of fear that had been growing and growing and growing...

She shuffled to the table, feeling like Happy. As if she were full of aches. But her body was okay. It was just her heart that hurt.

"I haven't heard from Trish for over two weeks. Her phone isn't working." Katie pictured Trish and her husband Gunner. Trish, short, thin and emotional; Gunner, tall, gaunt and cerebral. Yet he loved to hunt, and he loved Trish and his boys. A contradiction like most people. The more Katie knew people, the more contrary they were.

"What about Gunner?" Sam asked. "Did you call him?"

"This morning I finally called the *Sacramento Times* and asked for Gunner. They said he hasn't worked there for more than four months. The paper's online now and they laid a lot of people off." She heard the confusion and hurt in her raised voice. "Four months and Trish never told me."

"She's like you that way, honey. She's proud. And Gunner..." Sam shook his head. "If pride were the Trump Tower, he'd be living in the penthouse."

Katie sank into a chair. Planting her elbows on the table, she dropped her forehead into her palms, her fingers splayed through her hair. When Gunner got his job in Sacramento, he hadn't hidden his glee. He'd called Miracle a place where people stagnated. As if his journalism degree made him better than his friends.

"Did you call their parents?"

"I called Trish's mom last week." She made a face. Trish's mom made rocks look talkative. "She didn't know anything. I don't think Trish talks to her or her brothers often."

Sam nodded, his mouth tight. Trish's mom babied her sons and tolerated her daughter. Not having a mother who treasured them had bonded Trish and Katie. Trish hadn't come home to visit her overly strict mother since her dad died three years ago.

"What about Gunner's parents? They're somewhere in Florida now, right?"

She nodded. "They're taking care of Gunner's grandparents. I called his mom. She said he and Trish and the family are doing well. She didn't mention his job, so I'm guessing she doesn't know about it."

"He's an idiot. Did you tell her?"

"I didn't want to worry her. I think she's having a hard time taking care of her parents." She scrunched her forehead. "I don't know what to do about Trish. Should I call the Sacramento police?"

Sam stood in one fast swoop. "I know a guy in Sacramento. Was in 'Nam with him. I still got a Christmas card last December, so he's probably alive yet. I'll give him a call and see what he can do."

Happy howled outside, her *Let me in!* call. Katie went on her tiptoes and hugged her father. "Thank you," she whispered. "You're the best."

On his way out, he let Happy in. She limped to her food bowl. It was empty, but she still sniffed for food and licked the empty bowl. Katie looked at the clock and served Happy her last cup of dog food for the day.

As Katie moved around, the tightness still coiled in

her stomach. The feeling that something awful was about to happen, something that no pie on earth could fix, was wrong was too strong to go away.

The phone rang and she whipped it to her ear. But Rose was on the line, not Trish. Gabe had already called Rose about the video, and she told Katie it was all right with her. He was putting something together for Rose and her to sign.

She didn't talk long, and Katie could tell by the too happy note in her voice that everything wasn't happy at all.

It felt to Katie as if no one she knew was happy. Even Happy wasn't happy anymore. Well, unless she was eating or sleeping or being petted.

Katie sighed. There was only one thing she could do to shake this mood. She headed to the cupboards and started grabbing the ingredients for her Everything Will Be All Right Pie.

When the pie was done, she would bring three pieces to Rosa—for her and her two sons because Katie knew they must be feeling confused and angry.

But the first piece Katie would eat. She needed to do something to ease the snake-twisting-in-her-gut sense that nothing would be all right again.

TWELVE

This wasn't the first time Gabe knew what a heavy heart meant, but as usual he ignored it. The full moon shone down on him, lighting flat stones that led to Katie's back door. He left his car in the driveway, glad she and her father had separate driveways. After their meeting this afternoon, Gabe wanted to avoid any awkwardness.

He rang the doorbell. Here he was again, he thought. Like a dog that remembered where he'd found a bone once and kept coming back in hope of finding another one.

She opened the door and stared at him, a probing look.

"Friend," he said.

"Friend of what?"

He laughed softly, lightness creeping back into his mood. "Friend and not foe."

She didn't laugh. Instead she scratched the side of her forehead, as if considering whether to welcome him in. Finally she stepped back, a wordless invitation as she still watched him, her expression unreadable, the air between them thickening. Humming. Crackling with heat.

"So," she said. They stood in the kitchen, so close he could see the dark blue rim of her irises. "You didn't call. Were you afraid I'd tell you not to come?"

"I just felt I should come here."

Her head tilted. "Sometimes I feel that I should do things. But if I wait, the feeling passes."

"Think of all the opportunities you missed."

"Think of all the trouble." The look she gave him was cool. "I thought of having a fling with you."

He laughed with surprise and delight. Warmth pooled inside him despite her cool look. "Did that feeling pass?"

"I'm not sure. Would you care for a drink?"

"What do you have?" He was in, and she hadn't answered him, but he wasn't going to push it. He could wait for the right moment before going after what he really wanted.

"Wine. Or rum. I use it in several pies. Apple raisin, pumpkin, pecan, walnut."

He agreed to the rum. She gestured him into her living room while she prepared the drinks. The light was on, and as soon as he walked in, he heard the soft snores of her Beagle curled next to a navy recliner with the footrest up. An open book lay on the table next to it. Beside that was an e-reader. Leaning over the recliner, he checked out the book, a man and woman on the cover clutching each other, the man shirtless.

He raised his eyebrows. Interesting choice of reading material.

Hearing her crossing the kitchen floor toward the living room, he headed to the small, three-cushion sofa that sat in front of the drapery-covered window. The best position to watch her enter the room, and the sofa had plenty of room for her to sit next to him. Room enough to lie on it, though not full out. For that, they'd have to go to the bedroom. Or the floor. Or the kitchen table.

Thinking about all the choices, he grew semi-hard.

He needed to turn his mind to other thoughts, but they all seemed to end up in the same hot and sweaty place.

She wore a Green Bay Packers sweatshirt and gray sweatpants, the color combination not the best choice, but the way she threw mismatched clothes together made him smile inside. Cherise would've hated that look, been horrified by it. But to Gabe it looked comfortable and cute, the way her snoring old dog was comfortable and cute. And it brought up an urge to touch her, hold her, kiss her. Really good urges that he knew were really bad ones. She wasn't the kiss and leave kind of girl. It was probably a good thing he'd be the one leaving soon. If he stuck around, he might do something really stupid.

"I talked to Rosa." He took the drink from her outstretched hand. "She said to put this one up and see how it goes before filming any more. I doubt one short video will do it. I'd rather film more. You really don't need her permission."

"Maybe not, but I want it. Rosa isn't normally cautious." Katie sat on the other end of the sofa, holding her own rum and cola drink. "Everything in her life is changing, and it makes her nervous. She's used to a rhythm in her days, and that rhythm is broken."

"She called me the day she left her husband, ready to forge ahead."

Katie shrugged. "Life doesn't add up like sums all in a row. Life adds up sideways. Like a recipe. You add this and that, and then you think how much wonderful another flavor would do inside. And it's like magic."

"She should listen to me. My idea is the magic ingredient."

"Maybe what's magic for you isn't magic for Rosa." A small frown line creased Katie's forehead. "She watched the cooking shows for years, and I think it's been festering inside her that if she had the chance, she could do it as well as the other chefs. And she could." She nodded sharply. "In fact, she could do better. "

"It would be a great way to show her husband that's he's a fool."

Katie made a rude sound. "He's been a fool for many years. The whole village knows it."

"His kids?"

She looked down, and he could practically see invisible barriers shoot up around her. "It's hard having a parent that behaves badly."

"You sound like you know something about it."

"It was a long time ago. My mom had...problems. I've lived with my dad since I was almost six, and I'm okay now." She gave him a tight smile. "We were talking about Rosa. She's afraid to change her dream. She doesn't know anything about videos. She's probably afraid it will be too much for her and she won't have any control."

"Everyone is afraid. Everyone worries they won't have control. Everyone is concerned that it might be too much for them."

"Even you?"

"When I was a kid, I almost died." He frowned. Now they'd reached his discomfort zone. "Something like that, it makes you feel you must be here to do big things."

"Yet here you are in a small village."

"This is temporary. I'm not staying here."

"I keep forgetting you're leaving soon." She looked down at her hands folded on her lap. "Two of Katie's boys are here. Her oldest is at a culinary school in New York. The second works in the restaurant she and her husband started. The third was working for him but quit when he found out what his father did."

"Good for him."

Katie nodded. "As long as Rosa's two sons are here, she won't leave. And unlike me, she's ambitious. She outdoes me by about one hundred to one. Compared to her, I'm a slacker."

"That's not true," he said.

She gave him a sharp glance. "You're just saying that."

"I'm not the kind of guy that just says things."

"When men want something, they all turn into that kind of guy."

He wanted to laugh but what she said was too close to the truth. He rested his arm on top of the backrest, his fingers about two inches from her hair. "What do you think I want?"

"The video."

"I didn't have to come here for that. Not tonight."

Her expression looked trapped. She picked up her drink, brought the rim of the glass to her mouth, sipped, then put it on the coffee table again and turned to face him, her chin raised defiantly. "You're a man and I'm not. I'd say you want the usual."

"Affection," he said.

"Sex," she said, and her defiant look morphed into an I-dare-you-to-lie glare.

A smile built inside his chest. "Connection with another person."

"Sex," she said, her glare lightening.

The smiled widened. "Companionship."

"Sex," she said, and now her eyes laughed at him.

Exhilaration fizzed inside him. He slid over to the middle cushion. "Affection," he repeated.

"Sex." Her voice turned raspy.

He slid his arm around her shoulders, watching her face carefully. As if she were a bird who might fly away any second.

Like a bird in a pair of hands, she trembled. Then she looked into his eyes. Her face softened. With a sigh, she seemed to melt against him, boneless, like Alice sliding down into Wonderland.

He leaned forward to catch her mouth with his and felt himself sliding, too. Sliding into her embrace. Sliding into her kiss. Mouth to mouth. Tongue to tongue. Chest to chest.

He held her tight, as if to keep them from slipping away from each other. Because what they were doing was a slippery thing, and anything could happen. The worst and the best.

She tasted like rum and smelled like vanilla. He wanted to lick her skin and see if it would taste as good as she smelled. Taste like pie. A Katie pie.

He moved down from her mouth, giving her small kisses along her jaw. She wrapped her arms around his neck and made small noises as he kissed down to her throat, his mouth above her pulse. She seemed so clean and so fresh. So pure in her heart and soul. But the way he felt right now was anything but pure.

She made a protesting sound and jerked away from him. Breathing heavily, she put her hands on her cheeks. "I told you that you wanted sex."

His mind howled. Howled loudly like a dog that had lost his nice, chewy bone. "What about you? What do you want?"

THIRTEEN

The silence stretched out too long, and her mind was blank. She needed a pie to answer this, but sometimes pie wasn't enough. Sometimes she needed more. Arms. A hard body. The thrust and pull of a man. Sometimes the need came upon her like the need for a lemon meringue pie, normally one of her least favorite pies, so overwhelming she felt she would die if she didn't get it.

And then when she did eat a piece, she would think *That's all? That's it?*

That's how men were for her. Every time.

The need was once again drawing her back to Gabe. All her body cared about was that it wanted him with an overwhelming hunger, the way a vampire wanted blood. If she didn't satisfy that sexual hunger, her soul would starve.

Yet after she had it, she was always left with a bitter taste in her mouth. Sex stopped the ache of the hunger, but it never satisfied her half as much as a plain apple pie like Gram used to make. Sex was always a disappointment.

While pie...well, pie never disappointed.

"Love?" he asked, staring at her. "Is that what you want?

Her heart thumped. Love? No! For one thing, he was leaving. And just the thought of leaving Miracle made her feel sick and lost and scared.

Even if he weren't leaving, she hardly knew him.

She stood. Her hands shook. Her body shook. As though an earthquake had traveled through the village when she wasn't looking.

"Not love. I just want you," she whispered, knowing when push came to shove—or man came to woman—it would be no different than the other times. But the knowledge didn't matter. Her body was in charge, and it was demanding this. Like a child having a tantrum in the grocery store, the hunger was voracious. Demanding. Taking over her mind and body. Probably because it had been unfed for too long. A sexual starvation. That's why she felt if she couldn't have him she would die.

"You're killing me," he said.

Oh God, she knew how he felt. "Then let me heal you."

He froze for an instant, looking at her as if she were a witch. It felt as if the world stopped for that instant. "I swear you told me that before."

"In your dreams?"

He shook his head, and the heat in his face lessened, his brow furrowed as though figuring out a math equation.

She could give him a math equation. One man plus one woman equaled pretty damn good fun.

Or at least it would get rid of the soul-itching *need* that shouted so loudly, *Feed me! Feed me now!*

"You should be the star in a video," she said. "Not me."

"Why?"

"You're...mesmerizing. You're like the sun."

He smiled slowly. Warming his face and eyes like the slow fire burning inside her. "Right now I feel as hot as the sun."

"So what are we going to do about all this heat?" she whispered.

"This," he said. His eyes lighting up even brighter, he took her hands in his and pulled her down onto his lap so she faced him, her knees spread on either side of his thighs. Their lips met, melded, loved.

Small sounds came out of her mouth and their upper bodies came together. His hands slid under her top and up her back. She murmured with satisfaction. Her skin loved the contact, the warmth of his palms and fingers making her nerve ends purr.

With a twist of his body, he toppled her onto the couch with her thighs still around him. Then he was on top of her, pressing down on her most sensitive spot as he kissed her again and again. She squirmed and pressed her hips up, wanting more. Much more.

She wanted everything.

His hands continued their caressing. Slipping up the sides of her ribcage and onto her breasts.

Small whimpers came out of her mouth. She pressed her hips up more and held on tight. If she kept this up, she would explode soon. Explode into a thousand pieces.

Then his lips left hers and she felt lost, disoriented. He rained small kisses down her face, then down her neck, and now she felt found. Wonderfully, amazingly found.

"I want to kiss every inch of your body," he murmured.

She moaned in need. She moaned in agony. Grabbing his shoulders, she pushed him up and away, though he resisted.

"Now," she said. "I want you *now*."

His face stilled and then tensed. He rolled off her,

standing on the carpet. Without a word, he unsnapped and unzipped his jeans. As if in an erotic dream, she slid from the sofa then pulled off her clothes. Usually neat, she tossed her pants and top onto the carpet. Her bra landed on the coffee table. Her panties on the chair across the room.

They both stood there, and she looked him up and down and tried not to think he looked better than she did. But it was the truth. His legs, arms and chest were leanly muscled. Though he didn't have a six pack, his stomach was flat. His package... Her breath sucked in, and her skin heated. No complaints there.

But more than anything else, his skin gleamed golden, making him look like a statue come to life.

Almost afraid, she reached out and touched his arm. "It feels real," she whispered.

He put his hand over hers. His blue eyes blazed. "It's all real." He drew her hand down over his hard pectoral muscle, his nipple drawing a line on her palm. The contact sent a current through her arm and downward.

Her hand went downward, too. Down over his ribcage, down over the flat stomach, then down onto his erection that twitched under her hand.

"Does that feel real?" he asked.

She braced her legs to keep from crumbling to the floor. Closing her eyes, she explored him while he explored her. He started with his hand on her shoulder. And then her breast. And then lower, between her legs.

His fingers were magic.

She felt so much and so deeply, she couldn't contain herself. Her body shook crazily, but still she didn't stop touching him and he continued to touch her and rub her and touch and rub her some more...

Oh God, oh God, this is wonderful.

Oh God, oh God, never stop.

He stopped. A protest mewled from her mouth, the need inside her raging. Her eyes opened to see him rolling on a condom. All she could think was *Thank you, God.* Though she suspected God didn't really have anything to do with *this.*

Before she could think any more crazy thoughts, Gabe grinned and stepped forward to kiss her again, bending her backward.

Then she was falling, a crazy, wild free-fall, clutching him tightly. They landed on the sofa and he was on top of her, her knees bent to keep her feet from dangling over the sofa arms.

"Are you ready?" he asked and his eyes, his beautiful eyes, were melting her. Everything about him was melting her, as if she were caramel about to drizzle onto crisp slices of apples.

"Yes. Yes, yes, yes."

He entered her laughing. A triumphant, glorious laugh. That same triumph swelled inside her. This was the most wonderful feeling in the world.

Immediately he found her G-spot, her joy spot, the fireworks-inside-her spot. She clenched him with her inner muscles and gave a little scream. Once, twice, three times, staring into his glowing eyes as he moved in and out, in and out, sliding along that same wonderful spot. She pushed up and her little scream escalated into a loud scream. Over and over, and it was wonderful, it was fabulous.

Then he collapsed on top of her, grunting and huffing. His skin slick and hot.

She reached up and curled her arms around him, holding him tightly. They remained clasped together. She felt the hammering of his heart, and she knew hers was thumping just as fast and furious. They held on to each other for moments as their thundering hearts slowed and an overwhelming tiredness slugged through her body.

With a sigh, she closed her eyes. It was like a fairy tale come true... Only it wasn't a prince she'd just made love with.

"You're my angel," she murmured. "My angel Gabriel."

FOURTEEN

The sleeping dog snored softly and the sleeping woman curled on the sofa moaned in her sleep.

Gabe stood by the sofa, his clothes on now but not ready to leave yet. It felt too right being here in this small house in this tiny village with this one woman. At the same time, the rightness unsettled him. He was a big city boy, and he had big city boy plans. This was a temporary place, a one-time gig.

A long sigh came from Katie, and it echoed the unspoken sigh in his mind.

"Shh." He tucked the throw he'd grabbed from the chair around her, as if she were a child.

Not that he'd imagined she was a child when he made love to her. But in his mind he saw a girl child. Thin and serious with brown hair, big eyes and a big heart.

He'd always thought it was her big heart that had kept him from dying.

If Katie was that girl.

He sat in the chair and watched her still profile. He didn't know how much time passed before he slowly stood. Slowly made his way through the kitchen to the back door. He locked it before he headed to the car where he slowly backed up.

His entire drive to the motel was spent in a state of suspension. Thoughts of *was she?* and *what if she was?* tumbled in his mind like rolled dice.

Inside the motel room, he got out his cell phone but hesitated before calling his mother. She didn't like to think of *that time*, the way many war veterans didn't like to think of the bullets that just missed them. She'd been so afraid. She never talked about it without saying, "It's all behind us now, thank God." And always with a fearful glance over her shoulder. As if death, a black shadowy beast, could jump up and steal him away if she weren't vigilant.

It wasn't ten yet and she'd probably be reading one of her romances, something she had in common with Katie. The phone connected and she answered on the second ring, sounding happy to talk to him. She talked about his stepfather and half-sisters while he sat on the end of the bed, the mattress giving.

"Are you back in Chicago?" she asked finally. "Come for dinner on Sunday."

"I'm still in Wisconsin."

"Not for long, I hope. You've been helping your friends for too many years. It's time you got on with your career."

"Mom, this isn't a friend, it's a client. I'm getting paid for this. It's part of my career."

"It's a job. You're building for them, not for you. If you went to L.A. today, none of those wedding videos would help you. Nor a cooking video. You may as well dig ditches."

"Mom—"

"Don't *Mom* me. First you're in Africa building a hospital—for *three* years. I was scared every night." Her voice rose. "You came back...different. And you end up being Cherise's go-to guy."

"It was a paying job." He grimaced. His mom had him there. Had him everywhere. Right now he didn't regret the hospital. Not with all the images of the happy-crying-laughing faces on the final project. The eyes bright with hope. That was something he was proud of. In his old age, he'd look at his copy of the finished movie and think, *I helped do a good thing.*

But along with the hopeful faces, he'd seen hopelessness. He'd seen cruelty. He'd seen earthquakes and floods that some of the Africans said were sent from the devil.

And most of all, he'd seen the worst that people could do to each other.

It broke his spirit.

The nine months estimate to build the hospital had taken three years. The healing of his spirit had taken longer.

"I never meant to stay with Cherise so long," he said, answering the only part he could.

"She was so needy. Always with a hard luck story. Don said she knew how to play you."

Gabe frowned. He hadn't stayed because of Cherise's hard luck stories. He'd stayed because he didn't care. He was skating by in life, and he used her as much as she used him.

"I knew what I was doing. She knew what she wanted."

"Yes, she wanted *you.*" A mama lion ferociousness sharpened her voice. She sounded ready to attack anyone who interfered with her children. Even when the child was thirty years old.

"Stop worrying, she's out of the picture. I'm coming back to Chicago soon."

"Where will you be staying?"

"A friend's place. Not Cherise."

"Another woman?"

Scratching his chin, he pictured his mom on her gold chair with her slippered feet on a hassock. Wearing pants with elastic now that she was a little stocky. She hated it, used to being one of the skinny girls who could eat anything and not gain an ounce. She kept warning him he was like her and he'd gain weight when he was her age. The one time he told her he wasn't worried because he wouldn't go through menopause, she'd shot back, "No, you'll go through man-o-pause."

His sisters had laughed so hard they cried. He and Don had just looked at each other, shrugged, then chugged their beers and turned back to watch the Cubs game.

No way was he telling her he felt more for a woman he'd only known for two days than one he'd lived with for eleven months. He could imagine her worry that he was making another mistake.

If he'd learned one thing from being so near death that he could feel its heat and smell its sulfuric breath, it was that he didn't want to spend his life worrying. And he sure didn't want to cause the people who loved him any more distress.

"Her name is Sylvia," he said. "She won't even be there. She's in Canada, filming a movie."

"A *real* movie?"

He rolled his eyes. "Yes, Mom, a real movie."

"You're rolling your eyes, aren't you?"

"No."

"Don't lie to me. I can tell by your voice. Yes, I know your videos are real. But it doesn't seem the same."

Gabe opened his mouth to lecture her on control and copyrights and making money off the videos for your whole life versus a filming job, but he bit the words off. That wasn't the reason he called.

"Listen, I need a name. Remember when I was seven and really sick, just before I went to the hospital? While you worked, you left me with the babysitter in the apartment building?"

"The bottom floor apartment in the front? I remember. Well, not her name. You know how bad I am with names."

"Not her. The little girl who used to sit with me."

There was silence on the other end. He imagined the blank stare on her face.

"I think she lived in the next apartment building or across the street." He rubbed his hand across his chin and mouth. It was all so long ago. He remembered parts of it so clearly. Other parts...it was like he was swimming through a thick fog. "She used to call me her angel Gabriel."

His mom laughed. He laughed, too. Embarrassed but smiling. "I know. Silly."

"Not silly. Yes, I remember her. She was so sweet. Too bad her mom was a piece of work."

"What do you mean?"

"She was on something. Drugs or alcohol. I heard she was with a lot of men. The poor girl wore the same clothes all the time. The babysitter—Janell, I think, it's all coming back—she used to wash the girl's hair. She told me that she wasn't getting paid, but she was afraid if she didn't take care of the girl, the mom would leave her alone in the apartment."

"What did the mother do?"

"I don't know. Waitress, I think. Why are you asking?"

"You remember the girl's name?"

There was silence on the other end.

"Mom?"

"Why are you asking?"

"I just am." He pictured his mother frowning, a suspicious look on her face. "Do you know what happened to her?"

"They left. Just after you were in the hospital that last time—" She stopped, her voice choked. "I was so afraid that you were...just so afraid."

"I know, Mom, I know." Memories rushed back. And the one memory. It was clearer than the others. While the other kids played, the girl sat with him in the apartment. Telling him he was the angel Gabriel, and angels never died. Angels flew around and had fun. And sometimes they helped the tooth fairy.

When he was in the hospital he told that to himself, over and over. And he would picture her. Small and thin. Pale blue eyes and a sad look to her face. Even her smiles had been sad.

If only she had tried to feed him pies, he would be sure she was the right girl.

His mom sniffed. A sound he'd hoped never to hear again.

"It turned out to have a good ending, so no need to cry." He blinked hard. "Her name. It was Katie, wasn't it?"

"It could've been. I'm not sure. I think she and the babysitter came to the hospital to see you."

His eyes closed, and he gripped the cell phone tightly. He'd been so sick then, heavily medicated. He'd forgotten so much. But his mother's words unlocked cells in his brain, and he could see the hospital room. See the walls, cream paint on the top half, green on the bottom. And he could see the girl standing by the bed, her expression serious.

"You'll be out of here soon," she whispered. "You're

an angel and other angels are watching over you and you'll be all right. Then you're going to grow up and marry a princess and be happy because God won't let his angels die."

"Have you met her?" his mom asked, bringing him back to the present.

"I might have."

"In that tiny village? Miracle or Magical? Did she say anything?"

"It's Miracle. I'm not positive it's her."

"Did you ask her about it?"

"I doubt she'd remember. The girl was a year or two younger than me. Five or six. This one lives with her dad. Her mother isn't in the picture."

"If it's the same girl, that's a good thing. Did she live in Chicago with her mom? That's something she'd remember."

"I don't even know how to ask her."

"I can't believe this. You, with more nerve than anyone I know. You, who will dare anything. What are you afraid of?"

"Snakes."

"Stupid. If you want to know, ask her."

"I will." He changed the subject, and they chatted about his half sisters for a few more minutes until she yawned and said she was falling asleep.

After the call ended, he stayed on the edge of the bed, frowning because he knew the real answer to her question, *What are you afraid of?*

If Katie was that girl...it would make a difference. She'd kept him from dying. She'd said he was her angel. But all those years ago, she'd been his angel. Her faith had kept him alive. Without her, he'd be dead.

He would owe her.

He wouldn't be able to walk away from her.

In his heart he knew Katie wouldn't leave Miracle. She was happy here, making her pies. Fulfilled and satisfied.

Not him. Filming the videos wasn't everything for him. It was just *one* thing. With YouTube and cable, there were new career opportunities for filmmakers.

He could do anything.

But not if he stayed here. He'd almost died once. And sometimes in Africa, he thought it could happen again.

If he stayed in Miracle, it would be another form of dying.

FIFTEEN

In the darkness before the sun rose and the moon lowered, as almost everyone else in Miracle except for a few cats and insomniacs slept, Katie baked pies, her fingers busy and her heart singing, her stereo playing country music.

When she was done with her orders, she realized that without paying attention, she'd made two extra pies. Her Goodbye Pie and her Welcome Home Pie.

As she drove to the truck stop just outside Tomahawk to drop off an order, the sky lightened and her mood darkened.

Something good was going to happen today.

And something very bad.

The pies were never wrong.

SIXTEEN

By mid-morning the air had warmed. Indian summer. More like spring than fall. Katie made a trip to her dad's pumpkin patch for four sugar pumpkins. She loved this time of year, still warm but with a freshness in the air, the leaves turning colors, and best of all, pumpkins and apples growing in their own garden and on their own trees.

Yet she was thinking of other places she'd traveled to with Sam: Disney World, the Smoky Mountains, Nashville, the Grand Canyon, San Francisco and California wine country. And, of course, places closer to Miracle: Wisconsin Dells and the fun she had on the water rides; Summerfest in Milwaukee, with its many bands playing music that made her giddy; and the Mall of America in Minnesota with all the stores. She was always glad she went but more glad to return home.

In her kitchen, she turned her attention to the pumpkins, pushing down the restlessness. She cut the pumpkins in half and was scooping out seeds when through the open window she heard the crush of stones beneath tires.

Happy was outside, and Katie rinsed her hands and hurried out—just in case her mostly blind and deaf dog wandered under the tires. That's what she told herself. But her heart accelerated, and she knew she'd been waiting for this.

The first sight that met her eyes was Happy in the back yard. Happy's nose lifted, smelling Katie, then her jaws opened in the oversized smile that had earned the undersized Beagle her name. She bounded toward Katie with the energy of a younger dog. As if she hadn't seen Katie in five days instead of five minutes.

Katie's second sight was Gabe getting out of the car with his wavy blond hair and his eyes shining at her. Looking at him, she felt like a flower that bloomed. Last night she'd bloomed quite a few times.

When she woke up this morning and he was gone, she told herself she was relieved. Her life was so good, and a man would just mix it up. Like putting a chili pepper in one of her pies.

Now she was thinking that a chili pepper might be just what she needed.

"Hey." His voice was different today. Gentle and serious.

"Hey," she said back, forcing herself to not try to read anything into his voice, his eyes, his body language. There were two pies and one man. She'd find out soon which one was for him. She bent to pet Happy but kept her gaze on him. "Did you just get up?"

He shook his head. "The video's on YouTube. Want to see it?"

A thrill shimmered through her as she straightened. "Yes," she said. "Yes." She wanted to say *a thousand times yes,* but it wasn't that kind of question. That was the kind of answer to a *Will you marry me?* question.

And if he asked so early, she would have to say no.

Then she might tell him to ask her later, when they knew each other better.

She turned and led the way inside, holding the door wide for Happy to scamper in. Katie's laptop was in the office that her grandmother had used as a bedroom in her later years, after her knees got too bad for her to make it to the bigger bedroom upstairs.

Katie powered up her laptop then moved back to let Gabe take over.

All this time, neither of them talked. Anticipation built inside Katie.

When he brought up the video, she sat in her chair and watched the credits while cheery music opened in the background with a familiar voice saying pie names to a happy tune.

"Is that you?" she asked.

One side of his mouth quirked up, one dimple indented. "You notice I'm not really singing. I've got to save money where I can." He nodded at the screen. "It's on."

She shifted her gaze to the screen. As she stared at her face, she covered her mouth with her cupped hands, feeling her eyes open wide, laughing into her palms a couple times.

She looked and sounded...different. Pretty. Interesting. Funny.

The video stopped and she turned to look at Gabe, her hands away from her face. Her mouth still in an O shape.

"You liked it," he said.

She laughed shakily and nodded. As soon as he left, she would run to her dad's house and show him.

"And look." He pointed at the number on the left side, just below the video. "It's got eleven views already."

She shook her head. "Is that from you and me?"

"Only the one from you counts. The rest are other people."

"By this evening everyone in the village will have seen

it."

"The entire 629 population?"

"I don't think the babies will watch it." She laughed and heard the notes of exhilaration. "Maybe the toddlers."

She stood, feeling euphoric, as if balloons were attached to her heels. Another laugh bubbled out of her mouth, and she launched herself at Gabe, her body meeting his, her arms sweeping around him. He stumbled back, stopping against the wall. She laughed, a different note in her voice now. Low and sultry. One she'd never heard before.

His blue eyes darkened. The color of the sky just before nightfall.

Her laughter stopped, the breath stuck in her throat. She tilted her face and leaned forward, her lips parted.

It was like coming home, and that's when she knew. Her Welcome Home Pie was for him.

Exultation filled her again. She would remember this day always.

Then his hands curved around her upper arms and tugged her away from his chest. His face...there was a blank look on his face, his emotions shut down.

Her heart drummed inside her. Shock hit her. She'd been so...

Stupid. Stupid, stupid, stupid.

"Well..." She stepped back yet she still felt the imprint of his hands on her arms as he'd pushed her away. Rejected her. "I suppose you want to get back to Chicago."

He frowned and looked down then up, his shoulders squaring. She turned away from him. Whatever he had to say, she didn't want to hear.

He didn't want her? Fine. Then he could get out of

her life. Without him, she would not wither and die. In fact, she might even call a friend and go to Tomahawk on Saturday night. Hit a bar or two.

"Don't go." His voice was low. Serious.

She snapped around. Did he think she was going to fall apart just because he wanted her for only one night? He was thinking of the wrong woman.

"This is my house," she said. "I'm not the one who needs to go anywhere. You are."

"I'm doing this all wrong. It's not what you're thinking."

She crossed her arms. He didn't have a clue what she was thinking. Like wishing Happy were younger and would sense her anger and hurt and bite him.

Though even when Happy was younger, that wasn't going to happen. She was too...happy.

"Then tell me what it is," she said.

"When you were young, did you live in Chicago?"

Her eyebrows contracted. "Have you been talking to Linda Wegner? That was many years ago. I hardly remember Chicago."

"We might have known each other."

Katie froze. The drumming of her heart started again. *Oh no. Oh no. It couldn't be.*

"Right after my parents were divorced, when I was five, I got pretty sick. Turned out I had leukemia. My mom was working as a receptionist in a lawyer's office. My dad's insurance paid most of the medical bills."

He paused and looked at her, as if expecting her to pick it up. She shook her head. *No, no, no.*

"My babysitter was in the building," he continued. "She took care of a half dozen or so neighborhood kids. The only one I remember was a thin little girl who used to sit and talk to me. Who used to call me..." He stopped.

Staring at her. Compelling her to answer.

Tears welled up in her eyes, but she would not cry in front of him. Would. Not. Cry.

"Angel Gabriel," she whispered, and the moisture in her eyes welled up over her bottom lid.

She turned her head. Not wanting him to see.

He pulled her to him. Holding her close, as if she were precious to him.

SEVENTEEN

"I'm alive." Gabe heard the huskiness his voice even as he tried to sound casual. But nothing about this was casual. Not now, and not then. "In perfect health. No need to cry."

Katie jerked out of his hold, and her chin swept up an inch. The picture of a woman more inclined to punch him in his stomach—or lower—than one who would cry.

Then she sighed and her shoulders relaxed. She even smiled, though it came out looking sad. "So you are. You were still in the hospital when my mother took me to my dad's house. I used to pray for you every night."

He felt a twist in his chest. "We both went through a bad time."

"And we both made it." She reached her hand up as if to touch his cheek then pulled back.

His own right hand itched. He imagined brushing her cheeks with his fingertips. Imagined cupping her face with his fingers and palm. Imagined her leaning into his hand and gazing into his eyes.

But his hand remained at his side, and he curled his fingers. "I *have* to go to Chicago."

The corners of her lips curved up, and her eyes looked at him with such compassion and understanding that his gut hurt. She stepped back. "You don't have to go. You're choosing to go."

He opened his mouth to protest, but she held up her

hand. "No explanations needed."

"I just want to tell you—"

"Don't." She walked backward, shaking her head. "Just don't. I'm good with it." She shrugged. "You're not my first merry-go-round ride."

She turned and headed into the kitchen, walking fast. He had the sense she was running from him. Running from her feelings.

He wished to hell he could run from his.

Leaving Miracle was the right thing to do. He could never stay and be happy. She could never leave and be happy.

Yet he followed her, not ready to hop in his car yet, as if he were leaving something undone.

When he entered the kitchen, she was putting a box on the counter. She glanced over her shoulder at him. "I have a pie for you. Don't worry about traveling with it. It will be okay without refrigeration."

"What kind of pie?"

"Peach and apple." She slid it in and he watched her back, the tilt of her head, the way her hair brushed the top of her shoulder blades and her jeans curved over her hips and her ass.

He wiped his hand across his forehead. He felt like he was fifteen again, staring at the *derrière* of Miss Bernard, the French teacher who was a former Indianapolis Colts cheerleader, as she wrote on the whiteboard. He and all the other boys, the classroom thick with the ache of young male appreciation.

The ache he felt now was multiplied too many times to count.

Katie turned around with a smile that didn't match the dullness in her eyes, holding the pie box to him. "Here."

"I shouldn't take it."

"I made it for you."

"Not the whole pie."

One side of her smile curved down, and she shrugged. "It happens often. I wake up and know what pie to make."

"That's right. The pie talks to you." He smiled as if making a joke out of it. "The apple-peach pie just appeared and said, 'Make me.'"

Her smile dropped altogether, and she looked at him out of somber eyes. "I don't usually call it an apple-peach pie."

He held in his breath. Waiting for her to continue. As if what she said next would tell him everything. The wisdom of the world in the form of a pie.

"I call it my Goodbye Pie." She shoved it at him. "Whenever I make it, someone leaves."

He took the pie box from her. "I'm coming back. This is just temporary."

"Don't. Just...don't. You should go now." Her lips twisted and her eyes...though they were dry now, her eyes wept with sadness.

He stood there. Robbed of voice. Robbed of action. The man who always thought of the right thing to do and say stared at her as if she'd smacked him in the face with the pie instead of putting it in his hands.

"Now." She pitched her voice low and hard and made it an order. "Now."

His footsteps heavy, he headed toward the door, robot-like. When he reached the back hall, he paused. "If Rosa decides the videos are a good idea, you'll still do them?"

"This is too complicated. I can't deal with it." Her voice distant, she averted her eyes and turned her back to him.

Feeling as if she'd slugged him in the heart, he took two more steps and opened the back door.

He'd just found the woman of his dreams, and she was all wrong for him.

And he for her.

There was only one thing to do. He stepped outside, on autopilot, not feeling hurt, his emotions numb except for the throb in his chest as if a hammer struck his heart with every beat.

The storm door banged behind him, and he headed toward his car. It was over. Life would go on. Time would pass. He would find someone else. She would find someone else. And this ache in his chest would go away.

EIGHTEEN

"I hate men." Rosa glared around her. In Mo's Place on a Friday night there were as many women and children as men, but a few men jerked back and blinked wildly under her glare, as if a laser beam had stung their foreheads.

Katie imagined that it would make Gabe laugh. Then, as she'd done at least a hundred times since he'd left two weeks ago, she told herself not to think of him.

"The hating men thing must be tough on you with three sons," she said.

"I don't think of my boys as *men*. They'll always be my babies."

Since two of Rosa's babies were in their twenties—and the oldest had asked Katie out just a few months ago—she gazed down at the deep-fried perch on her plate. Not her favorite but it was the best pick from the Friday Night fish fry menu. Mo never tried to pass off his food as anything more than bar dining. He'd bought the Amber Waves of Grain bar a couple months ago, changed the name, expanded the menu, added a karaoke stage, and was slowly turning it into a community gathering spot instead of a place where mostly men drank beer, played darts, talked loudly, and according to Linda Wegner, did other disgusting things.

"So, have you heard from Gabe?" Rosa wrinkled her nose at the fish and picked up a sweet potato French fry.

Mo's was known for their sweet potato French fries and the sweet potato pies. The fries were by Mo, the pies by Katie.

Katie swallowed a bite of perch before answering. Her throat was tight and she had to take two gulps of water to make it go down. "No."

"I thought you two had something going on."

"He's a city boy. I'm a country girl."

"I think that was a song," Rosa said.

Katie shrugged. "Life in songs usually ends better than in real life."

"In real life," Rosa said, "husbands cheat with a woman half your age and are too stupid to use birth control."

"In real life," Katie said, "a man can make love with you one night then leave you the next day."

Rosa's gaze flicked up to Katie. "Is that what happened with you and Gabe?"

"Of course not." This time Katie picked up her wine and took a sip. When she finished, Rosa was giving her The Stare. When Rosa gave The Stare, she reminded Katie of Mother Nature. Lying to Mother Nature was not a good thing.

Katie sighed and shrugged. "Maybe."

Rosa narrowed her eyes. "Men." The word was thick with dislike. "They're pigs."

"I don't hate Gabe." Katie took another sip of wine. She missed Gabe, but it wasn't the first time. A long time ago—or so it seemed—she had missed the boy Gabe. For years, she wondered what happened to him.

She had missed him more than she missed her mother.

"You're too nice," Rosa said.

"I knew him before."

Rosa stared at her, frozen in place with a fry halfway to her mouth. "Why didn't you tell me?"

"I didn't find out until the morning he left. It was in Chicago where I lived with my mother before she dropped me off at Sam's and said, 'Guess what? Here's your daughter.'"

"Did she really?" Rosa's eyes were big. "I heard that story, but I thought it was exaggerated."

"It's kind of blurry. That's about all I remember." But it wasn't. She remembered Sam crouching so his long face was level with hers, telling her she looked just like pictures of his mom when she was Katie's age, and he was happy to get to know her. Then her grandmother was there, crying over her, hugging her and saying how beautiful she was.

Sometime during all the hugging and crying, Katie's mom had left. Driving away from Katie as fast as she could. With Katie turning to run after her. Screaming, "Mommy! Mommy!"

"Anyway," Katie continued, "when we were in Chicago, one of our neighbors ran a mini daycare in her apartment."

"I'm sure that was illegal."

"And I'm sure it was cheaper than a licensed daycare. I don't remember the woman in charge, I just remember Gabe. He had leukemia and was pretty sick."

Rosa made a soft noise of sympathy, her features softening.

Katie nodded. "I know. So when I think of Gabe, I'm just glad he's alive."

"You're a better woman than I am," Rosa said. "I'd still want him to walk along the city street, not notice one of the sewer covers was missing and fall into it."

Laughter bubbled up in Katie, but it quickly turned

into a smile that she didn't feel. "I try to avoid anger." Besides, she didn't have room for anger. Or regrets or sadness. Though like dustballs, the unwanted emotions gathered in the corners of her mind when she wasn't looking.

Rosa shrugged and gave her *good luck with that* grimace. "How's the video doing?"

"It has over nine hundred views." Katie laughed, pushing away the remnants of sadness. "I know it's mostly people from Miracle and some from my Tomahawk customers, but I feel good."

"You'll get more." Rosa reached over and touched the back of Katie's hand on the table. A motherly touch, her face beaming with pride, as if Katie were her daughter.

Katie blinked then beamed back. "It doesn't matter. At this rate it will be a loooong time before anyone wants to do advertising on my video."

"That's because it's just one," Rosa said. "You need more. Gabe needs to come back and film you. I don't mind if you do the short videos."

Sadness stirred inside Katie again. "It's better that I don't make anything with him."

"Men." Rosa scowled. "If only they'd think with their minds instead of their lower parts, the world would be in a better place."

Katie's laughter was hollow, and she pushed her dish away. She didn't even want any of her sweet potato pie. She wanted something light. Something happy. With strawberries or even key lime. Both cheery, light pies. Pies that said *Life is good.*

"What about the pilot? Any bites?" Katie nodded at Mo who stopped at the next table to chat with the Miller sisters. Mo was in his upper thirties, Katie guessed. She wasn't sure where he came from or why he was there.

Linda Wegner was telling people he was hiding out from the Mafia, something Katie suspected she made up because of his New Jersey accent. No one with any sense believed her.

Rosa shook her head and made a face. "I'll have to get a job, but there's nothing for me here. I'll have to go to Oshkosh or Tomahawk, and I hate driving in snow."

"Cook at my place. You can do what I do. Make your cannelloni and your other dishes. Deliver them to restaurants."

"It works for pies," Rosa said. "Not food. I can't see—"

"Work for me." Mo leaned over their table, his expression intense. "My business is growing. And with you here..." He swept out his arms, missing Katie's head by an inch. "The sky's the limit."

"Compete with Fabrini's?" Rosa shook her head again though less firmly this time. "I don't know—"

"Not Fabrini's." Mo gestured again, as if throwing her comment away. "I'm not aiming for the fine dining crowd. I want the working crowd." He cocked his head. "I've been to Italy."

Rosa raised her eyebrows. "Me, too." Her accent, usually not noticeable, thickened.

"You know the little cafes, where you can just have pasta and sauce and a meatball?" He steepled his surprisingly small hands under his chin and closed his eyes in the silent, appreciative prayer that Katie often felt about her pies. Then his lids opened and he leaned down again, his mouth inches from Rosa's. As if he were her lover.

Around them, the sound level dropped. Katie could feel about thirty pairs of eyes on their table.

"That's what you and I can do. Delicious and fast."

"And cheap," Rosa said.

Grinning, he nodded, smile lines on his sallow face making multiple parentheses. "And cheap."

"I still want to be a chef on a TV show."

"Knock yourself out."

Her eyes narrowed. "I'll come by tomorrow and talk about money and hours."

"You got it, babe." He slapped his hand on her shoulders, stood, grinned as if he'd won the lottery, then swaggered to the bar.

The noise level rose as if everyone in the bar area talked at once.

"Wegner's is going to be busy tomorrow," Katie said. "Are you really doing this? You have other options."

Rosa laughed low in her throat. "You know why I have to do this?"

Katie shook her head, though she guessed.

"Mike is going to hate it."

"Ahh." But Katie didn't think that was the only reason. She'd seen the way Rosa and Mo looked at each other. As if they wanted to throw spaghetti sauce on each other's bodies then lick off every inch.

"You like him, don't you?" Katie asked.

"Mo?" Rosa shrugged, and her smile was like a shrug, too. "I'm not sleeping with my boss again. That's how I married Mike. I'm older now, and wiser."

"I don't think Mo is like Mike."

Rosa put her elbows on the table and leaned forward. "Maybe not," she said, her voice pitched low, her expression serious, "but when you work for someone else, they always think they're the boss. Especially if they have Italian blood in them."

Katie's cell phone trilled, and she dug her phone out of her purse. The phone number on the display was local, but no name showed up. She put it to her ear and clicked on *Talk*, expecting a pie order.

"Hi, Katie, guess what?"

Katie sat up straight. "Trish! What happened to you? I've been so worried."

"You don't have to worry anymore. I'm home."

NINETEEN

Thirty was too old to be a disappointment to your parents, Gabe thought as he led his mom and stepfather into the apartment where he was staying until he found his own place. Don took in the pink, purple and turquoise colors and he looked as if he wanted to be somewhere else.

Gabe's mother, Heidi, furrowed her forehead. "What are you doing now?"

The question hung in the air so heavy that Gabe thought he might glance up and see a giant question mark hanging from the high ceiling. "Getting you coffee."

He had to turn his back on her. What she wanted him to be was something he wasn't ready for. Not now. Maybe not ever.

When Gabe returned to his parents with their coffees, he wanted to tell Heidi he was sorry he disappointed her, but he held back the words. She would deny it even as she looked at him with her forehead puckered with worry. He'd seen that look too often.

"I'm freelancing," he said. A euphemism for doing wedding gigs. Not for Cherise—that hadn't ended well and he wasn't going back to her. He'd also filmed videos for two budding comics. The comics weren't very good yet, but they wanted it and were working at their craft. When they got better and had a following, there was a chance they'd want him to film them again.

Right now he felt rudderless, spending his days talking to friends, getting ideas. When he'd first seen Katie and Rosa's pictures three weeks ago, he'd felt the fire in his belly. But now...the fire had damped down with every mile that he'd driven away from Miracle.

As if his miracle was back in the village he'd sped away from.

"Anything you can show us?" Don asked.

"The cooking video," Heidi said. "I want to see it."

"Rosa's shopping the cooking show around, but I did a three-minute video with the younger one." Gabe headed for his laptop on the tiny dining table near the kitchen end in the open concept living area. "I'll bring it over to you."

"We'll watch it at the table," Heidi said, and Gabe heard the sofa creak as they got to their feet. "It will be better to see it there."

"Isn't that what the Big Bad Wolf said to Little Red?" Don asked.

"Don! Will you stop?"

By the time they reached Gabe, the video was up. He didn't look behind him, too busy staring at the small image of Katie's face and feeling as if a hand reached inside his chest and squeezed his heart.

Then his parents were leaning to peer at the screen as he took a deep breath and told himself whatever he was feeling, he'd get over it.

"You sit," he got up and stood behind them. "I've seen it before."

It must've been the mother thing, because Heidi shot him a *something's wrong* look. But Don sat and so did she, more slowly. Gabe leaned between them to click on the video. As he straightened, the video started with Katie's nervous smile and scared eyes that hurt Gabe to look at. "I'm Katie Guthrie," she said, "and I make pies."

Then his voice, the unseen interviewer, advised her to pretend she was talking to her lovers, and she responded by saying she didn't tell her lovers how to make a pie, she baked the pies for them.

His parents chuckled and he had to look at them, away from the screen because he didn't want to show his emotions in front of his mom. That's when he saw they were bending forward, grinning, listening to Katie talk, fully involved.

The video only lasted two minutes and forty-two seconds, but Gabe counted the laughter: ten times for his mom and twelve for his easygoing stepdad. Not loud, belly-grabbing laughs, but chuckles. And when they weren't chuckling, smiles stretched across their faces.

After it ended and the credits rolled across the scene, he was sorry. He wanted these few moments to stretch longer.

"Oh, look! There's your name!" His mom pointed, sitting back. She glanced over her shoulder at him. "I enjoyed that. You should do more of it."

"I'm waiting for the right project."

"You've got the right project." Don jabbed a finger at the screen. "It's got almost three thousand views. A lot more than Ash and Ally's videos. That's good, isn't it?"

"It hasn't gotten viral yet, but the views are growing." Pride rose in him, a bitter-sweet feeling. He wondered if Katie looked at it every day. Wondered if she cared about the views.

"Why not do more videos with her?" Frustration edged Don's voice.

"That's her, isn't it?" Heidi looked at Gabe with pity in her eyes. "The girl from the babysitter's. The one who came to the hospital."

Gabe shrugged. "It's her."

Heidi stood, and Don got up, frowning as if he were trying to understand what they were talking about.

"Is that why you've changed?" Heidi asked. "Is that why you're different?"

"Yeah, I noticed, too." Don shook his head. "You were always so calm and confident. Now you're...I don't know." He peered at Heidi. "You're better at this stuff. What's he like now?"

"In love," she said, and her face softened. "He's in love with the girl."

The words were like blows, and Gabe turned his head away, then turned back. Some things he couldn't run away from. "It'll go away."

"She doesn't love you?" Indignation sparked in Heidi's voice.

"I don't know." He didn't want to know. "We want different things out of life. We'd be miserable together."

Don clapped his hand on Gabe's shoulder. "You're right. You'll get over this. It just takes time."

Heidi put her hand on his other shoulder, looking at him with tears in her eyes. "You'll get it together. I know you will. You've gotten over worse, haven't you?"

"And you'll soon find what you want to do," Don said.

His mom frowned. "You know what's so interesting about the girl?"

Gabe kept his mouth shut. How could he pick out one thing? To him she was interesting when she scratched Happy behind her floppy ear. When she was nervous of the camera. And when she was naked. Then she was *very* interesting.

"She loves what she does," Heidi said. "That's always interesting."

"You're right." Don slid his hand on the back of

Heidi's neck.

"I'm always right." She and Don laughed, sharing a meaningful look before she turned back to Gabe. "Maybe pies aren't the most important things. Not like building a hospital or catching murderers, but she has a *passion* for it. That's why I liked watching her. Her passion and love shines through everything she says. You should do more of that."

Looking at them, the two of them in perfect harmony, he *knew*. His mojo. It was here, right in front of him. Not the whole picture, but a little piece of it.

Telling Heidi and Don to wait, he headed for his camera. There was no sound man around, but he set up the boom himself, telling them to sit on the couch. He checked the sound and the lighting. Made adjustments. Finally he was ready.

"What do you think is love?" he asked.

TWENTY

"I live on a farm, not in a barn," Trish's mother's stern voice scraped into the kitchen with the gleaming white appliances and the black and white squared vinyl floor that Katie remembered from her childhood, as spotless as ever.

Watching Trish put tea bags in two mugs filled with microwaved water, Katie winced and wished she could bake a pie that would cure Mrs. Brauer's OCD. But though her pies made people feel as if the world wasn't a bad place, they didn't cure diseases or meanness.

The TV went on. Katie peered into the living room to see Mrs. Brauer glare at Trish's two boys then head to her bedroom. Katie grimaced and turned back to her friend. Trish was a good six inches shorter than her and she used to be a wisp of a girl. She still had stick-figure arms and legs, but her belly stuck out like she'd swallowed a small blimp.

"What's wrong?" Katie asked.

"Nothing." Trish handed Katie a mug. They both stood by the fake wood counter. "I'm six and a half months pregnant."

"How many?"

"You can tell?"

"It was either that or you ate a baby whale." Katie forced herself to keep her eyes on Trish's face instead of her belly.

Trish's mouth turned down. "Quads."

"Four." Katie put her mug on the counter to keep from dropping it. Holy coconut pie! Katie couldn't imagine having six dogs in her house much less six kids.

"And we didn't use any drugs," Trish said.

Katie stepped back. "I never thought you did."

Trish rolled her eyes. "You wouldn't believe how many times people asked me that in California. I used to think I should wear a big sign when I went to the market, like on organic chicken packages, saying it was all natural, no additives, no fillers. Free range." She smiled crookedly. "It wasn't even supposed to happen. We were using birth control."

"Whatever happens, I've got your back."

"Good thing you've got my back, because my stomach's already covered." She patted the top of her belly. "I feel like I'm carrying a Boy Scout Troop."

They both laughed, but it sounded hollow. "Why didn't you tell me before?" Katie asked.

"I felt so..." Trish frowned and shook her head. With dark circles under her eyes, she looked haunted. "Things weren't going well. Gunner was laid off. He tried to find a job, but there weren't any. His work insurance ran out. We *had* to pay it ourselves—so much can go wrong with quads. But our money was running out." Her lips curved down. "So was our pride. We packed up and drove back to Miracle."

"Oh, sweetie." Katie felt her own mouth and eyes sag into a sad face. That wouldn't help Trish's morale, and she grabbed the box she'd set on the counter when she entered the kitchen. "For you."

Trish smiled crookedly again. "Let me guess. Animal, vegetable, mineral or pie?"

"Mineral."

"Liar." Trish was opening the box already, bending over to see the flaps better, her fingers busy. "I'm probably not supposed to eat this, but I will anyway. What do you call the pie?"

"A Welcome Home Pie. It might be a little frozen still. I took it out of the freezer this morning."

Trish stopped pulling the pie out of the box and stared at her. "When did you make it?"

"Two weeks and two days ago."

"That's when we decided to come home. You're spooky."

"Am I? Then maybe you want to give me back my spooky pie."

"No way, José." Trish turned back to the box and drew the pie out. It was a two crust, and she turned to Katie with her eyebrows up. "What is it?"

"Pumpkin apple pie." Katie made a face. "That's why I didn't think it was for you. I know your favorite is French silk."

"My favorite used to be French silk. It changed. Now it's apples and pumpkins. You know what you are? A pie psychic?"

"I guess that's better than being a pie whisperer."

"I think you're that, too."

"This pie psychic says that before you serve it, you should probably put it in the oven for about ten minutes on 300 degrees."

"Or I could put it in the microwave for one minute."

Running footsteps came from the living room, and at the same time a car door slammed outside.

"What do you got, Mom?" The two boys both resembled their sturdy, brown-haired dad. The six-year-old was only a couple inches taller than his brother, but the four-year-old still had the toddler freshness on his face.

"Nothing." Trish turned to stand in front of the pie.

The boys separated, like water in a river splitting to go around a large boulder. "Pie!" they shouted at the same time.

From deeper in the house, a door slammed and Trish winced. Then the back door opened and Gunner walked in, took one look at Katie and grinned.

"Hey, girl," he said. "You look the same. I think you have flour on your top."

"Welcome home," Katie said. "And thank you for pointing out my poor grooming."

"Dad! We've got pie," the oldest boy said. "I don't know what kind it is."

"Doesn't matter. If Katie made it, it's delicious." Gunner raised his brows. "You got a man yet?"

"After knowing you? Who could compete?"

Trish laughed and the boys giggled. Gunner stilled, looking at them. His face...it seemed to Katie that it filled with hurt and love and sorrow and more love. He put his hand on Trish's belly.

"C'mon, boys." He gestured to them, and the boys stopped reaching for the pie and stepped in front of Trish. They placed their smaller hands on Trish's belly, one on each side of their dad's. Staring from him to their mother.

"We're going to make it," he said.

"We're going to make it," the boys said loudly, the youngest shouting.

Trish spread her hands over theirs, connecting all four of them. "We're going to make it," she whispered. "All eight of us."

Tears warmed Katie's eyes, and her throat ached. She felt like an intruder. She took a step back, and Trish smiled at her, lifting her hand. "Let's have pie," she said.

They insisted Katie have pie, too. There were only four chairs, and she and Gunner fought over who would stand. Gunner won, and when Trish cut the pie the boys stared at the pieces, as if they hadn't had a treat in a while.

It occurred to Katie that maybe they hadn't. Not if things were so bad. The stupid ache returned to her throat, and she sat. Even if she could talk without sobbing, she couldn't think of anything to say that would make things better.

"I got a job," Gunner said.

"Good." Trish's mother appeared in the entryway from the formal living room without any warning, and Katie jerked back, having forgotten that freaky trick of Mrs. Brauer's. "That means you'll be able to leave soon."

The boys stared at their grandmother, their faces showing their shock and fear.

Trish set her fork down, her face paling two shades.

Gunner's face turned red.

Katie stood, a pulse in her neck throbbing. "They can leave right now," she said, hearing the winter coldness in her voice, a reflection of the iciness in her heart. She glanced around the table at her friend and her family, their faces shocked, and her heart warmed with love for them. "You're coming to my place."

TWENTY-ONE

Heidi had to comb her hair before allowing herself to be filmed. She came back with her lips a bronze color, complaining that she didn't have any other makeup on, and at least he should've warned her.

Don called her a diva. She punched his arm, and he decided he needed to comb his hair. She called after him, "Who's the diva now?"

Gabe double-checked to make sure the lighting was flattering. If it wasn't, his mom would complain for the next forty years.

Finally they sat on the turquoise couch. He played the off-screen moderator again, repeating, "What do you think love is?"

Heidi looked at Don. "I'll answer first." He nodded, and she turned to Gabe, leaning forward slightly to look straight at the camera, though it wasn't necessary. "Love is action."

"What does that mean?"

"It means being there for the other person." Her gaze flickered to him. "It means sitting at the bedside of your dying child and praying and loving. And when you're there for him..." Tears gathered in her eyes and she pressed her lips together. After a second, she inhaled and continued, "When that happens, all the other little things that used to bother you so much...none of it matters.

Only this boy matters." She pointed at him, and the tear swelled over her lower eyelid and slid downward. "And when a miracle happens, when he gets better..." She stopped to swallow, then gave him a trembling, watery smile.

"Do you want to break?" Gabe asked.

She shook her head and looked at the camera again. In a whisper, she said, "That's everything."

Don leaned sideways, out of camera range, but Gabe didn't follow him. He kept the focus on Heidi as she smiled at him with her glistening eyes and her trembling mouth.

Then Don was back, handing Heidi a handful of tissues. While she patted her cheeks and blew her nose, Gabe shifted the camera focus to him.

"What's love to you, Don?"

"That's easy. Love is your mom and your sisters and you. You all mean everything to me." His voice lowered. "I'm one of the lucky ones that enjoy what I do for a living. But that's not my happiness or my life. They are." He paused, frown lines creasing his forehead. As if he made up his mind, he craned his head toward the camera. "I never told you this, but I come from a family that was very strict. They rarely hugged. My mom was depressed and on medication. My dad was in sales, traveling most of the time. When he was home, he would spend most of the time with his buddies."

Heidi rubbed his shoulder. "You're a great dad and husband."

"I didn't want to be like him." He spoke to Heidi now. "I didn't want to be like either of them."

"You're nothing like them. *Nothing*."

They clasped each other and held on tight, as if they were holding onto life itself, their eyes closed tight.

Gabe waited a few seconds, then turned off the camera and set down the boom. Only then did he sit back in his chair, stunned. And something more. Uplifted.

This is it. This is what I need to do.

Show the heart of people. The best of them...and sometimes the worst of them.

He didn't know what or how...

But where... His heart thumped. He knew the place, though dammit, it was a place he'd sworn to never return. A place where emotions were raw and tears sometimes flowed like blood.

TWENTY-TWO

Tears stuck in her throat, Katie trudged home down the country road. It was sunny out, warm for late September—the weather changing wildly every few days—but in her heart it was dark and cold.

This wasn't supposed to happen in Miracle.

She didn't cry. Tears didn't come easily to her. She suspected she'd held back tears too much when she was young because she didn't know what her mother would do. And then she was in this new place where people loved her. Afraid to cry here. They might think she didn't appreciate them, and maybe they would get mad at her.

When she realized it wasn't going to happen, that they loved her even when she made noise or dropped something by mistake, and when her dad and grandmother didn't expect her to stay in a corner and not make too much noise and not bother them, then she had no need to cry.

That was a long time ago. Of course sad things had happened since then. Her grandmother's death. Katie had cried then. She missed her. And just this last year, a lot of sad things had happened. Not just to her, but to everyone.

Or was it always happening, and she was finally at the age to notice?

She was kicking a small rock in the road when a bark brought her head up and she spied a tall man in black jeans and a navy T-shirt striding her way. An unleashed English Setter raced toward her. Katie's spirits, as low as the cut corn on the side of the road, lifted as she held her arms out to the Setter with its mouth open in a big smile.

"Tuck." She crouched down.

Forty-five pounds of dog raced into her. Laughing, she fell back onto her butt, hugging the dog's neck. Tuck licked her chin as she grinned up at her father who gazed down at them indulgently.

She kissed Tuck's nose, then scrambled to her feet. As she brushed dirt off her backside, her lightheartedness melted away. Her dad was holding a square pan. He wore sunglasses, and the sides of his face creased in a smile.

"I guess you saw Trish and Gunner already," he said.

"Dad, it was awful." A big ball of hurt in her throat made it hard to talk, and she swallowed. "Trish is going to have quadruplets, Gunner lost his job, and now Mrs. Brauer says they can't stay at her place anymore. I offered my house, but Trish said no. They're going to see if there's someplace they can rent."

"You only have two bedrooms," Sam said.

"I could sleep at your place."

"You could. But with quads, they'll need more rooms soon."

"I know." She frowned, thinking what Trish said about quads coming early and all the problems she might have. "They kept their insurance. I think it costs a lot."

"At least Gunner has a job now."

"You heard?" She rolled her eyes, not at him but at herself. Of course he heard. This was Miracle, the place where gossip made an Indy 500 race look slow. "Never mind. I doubt Earl will pay for their insurance. It's going to be a while before they can afford a home." She shook her head. "What's wrong with Mrs. Brauer? I know it's a full house, but why doesn't she have Trish's brothers go somewhere else until Trish and Gunner find a home?"

"She probably has her reasons. Tim takes care of the farm."

"Ben doesn't. And he must make decent money as a paramedic."

"It will work out." Sam gestured with the square pan, and Katie squinted at it.

"That's your brownies, isn't it? You're not bringing that over to Mrs. Brauer's."

"I am."

Putting both hands on her hips, she narrowed her eyes. "It's got weed in it, doesn't it?" The fact that her dad grew weed for his recreation and a bit extra for anyone who needed medicinal help was probably the best kept secret in Miracle. "Mrs. Brauer is going to have a fit."

"No, she won't." He lifted his sunglasses, and his eyes didn't have their usual smile. "Honey, it's for her. She asked me to bring it."

She jerked back. "Is she sick?"

"Terminal."

"Shit."

"Yeah, that's the word."

"Cancer?"

"Colon. She's not going in for chemo. Far as I know, she hasn't told anyone but me."

Tears burned Katie's eyes. "The miracle that was prophesied, maybe it will be for her, and she'll live."

He shrugged. "You have to hope for a miracle to get one. Mrs. Brauer doesn't hope for anything."

"Except something to ease the pain." Katie nodded at the brownies. "So that's why she needs Tim and Ben. Ben will take care of her at the end."

"I expect so. Trish and Gunner will work something

out."

"How?" Katie heard the way her voice shook. Her dad was so smart and so calm. When she first met him and in his deep, resonating voice, he told her she was his child, she thought he was God. But it was more than his voice; it was the calm inside him, the sureness, as if he saw everything—the good and the bad—and didn't judge.

That outlook made her want to do better. She thought it made everyone who spent time with him want to do better. Maybe that was why the news about his illicit crop never made it out of the village. Besides, everyone in the village knew someone who used it to help them through a bad stretch.

"How?" she repeated. "How will Trish and Gunner manage?"

His eyes seemed to bleed sadness. "I don't know, honey."

"Neither do I. But she's my best friend, and I have to do something."

TWENTY-THREE

The car seemed to drive itself to the hospital. Gabe parked in front of it, across the street, and stared, ignoring the *No Parking* sign. Gabe had thought he remembered the hospital, but in his mind it was cleaner and more solid. Now it looked browner and shabbier. As if he remembered a strong young man and now he was looking at a shuffling old man.

The dead feeling he'd had for so long seeped back. He put the car in gear to leave when a bus pulled up a short way ahead of him. In the side view mirror he could see traffic coming. Relaxing, his hands still on the steering wheel, he watched the passengers step onto the sidewalk. First a heavy woman wearing sneakers. Her purposeful stride in her sensible shoes as she headed to the crosswalk in front of him made him think she was a nurse. A couple seconds later a thin older man with a cane hobbled off the bus. Behind him came a boy with a cap and a woman whom Gabe guessed was his mother.

As the mother-son duo neared Gabe, he saw that where there was no cap there was no hair.

Gabe's body reacted before his thoughts. He jerked the key out and hopped out of the car then strode toward the boy and the woman.

"Hi," he said. "I'm Gabe Robbins."

"I'm Scott," the boy said. He was about eight, Gabe guessed. The mother clutched her son's hand, her eyes narrowed in suspicion.

"Do you have a moment to talk?" Gabe asked the mother. "I can go inside with you, if you like." He pointed at the hospital and looked down at Scott. "As a kid, I was a patient, so I know how long you have to wait to get anything to happen."

"*Forever,*" Scott said, with feeling in his voice.

Gabe looked at the mother again, as a person this time instead of the boy's mother. He got a quick impression: dark hair, short, chunky, a small nose, no ring, her only jewelry a thin silver necklace with a heart-shaped locket. Gabe would bet money it showed a picture of Scott. She made him think of a teacher or a librarian, though she could've been anything.

"I can give you the name of my doctor." Gabe focused his attention on the mother. "He seemed old to me back then, though he was probably in his late twenties. Last I heard, he was still practicing here."

"What did you have?" the mother asked.

"Leukemia."

"And you lived?" Scott looked at him with wide eyes.

Gabe glanced down. "It's not my ghost you're talking to. Do you have leu—"

Scott shook his head, stopping Gabe.

"Brain tumor," the mother said, the words slow, as if they were dragged out of her.

"My last roommate had leukemia," Scott said.

"I make movies and videos." Gabe took out his wallet and drew out a card. "You can look up my website. Or I can get my laptop out if you have time. I can show it to you."

The mother took the card, glanced at it then back at him, still radiating distrust. "What do you want from us?"

"I want to film Scott and ask him a few questions. There's a video I put on YouTube. It's about pies, but you can see what I'm talking about. You have a few minutes? I can show it to you."

"We're early." The boy tugged his mom's coat. "Say yes. I want to look at it."

The mother's indecision last for only seconds before she pointed to the bench by the bus stop. "We can look at it there. I'll give you fifteen minutes, then we have to go inside."

Gabe picked up his laptop. When he turned back, the mother was holding Scott's hand and standing slightly in front of him. Gabe didn't blame her for being wary. That was the kind of world it was.

The three of them crossed to the bus stop bench. Once there, Gabe fired up the computer and typed in his website URL. He could've gone straight to YouTube, but he wanted the mother to see he was legit. Only then did he play Katie's video.

The two watched almost in silence, but their expressions changed, a wide smile for the boy, a small one for the mother. A laugh from the boy, a chuckle from the mother. When it was over, Scott looked at his mom. "I want a piece of pie."

His mom curved her hand on Scott's shoulder. "Me, too." She turned her gaze to Gabe. "We have ten more minutes. What do you want?"

"Just to film Scott answering questions. Something similar to the pie baker's video. It might help other kids." He gestured. "We can do it here right now. You can sit next to him. I'll send you a release form and until you sign it, I won't post the video anywhere."

"I want to do that," Scott said. "Please, Mom. I'd like that."

His mom looked at Gabe for what seemed like minutes but was probably only seconds. Then her tight shoulders loosened, and Gabe relaxed, ready to hurry to his car before she said yes.

It took Gabe seven of the ten minutes setting up the camera and the lighting and fixing the boom. A kid about seventeen stopped and said he did that for a band. Gabe asked if he'd handle the boom, saying he'd put him down as the sound guy when it went live, and the kid said sure.

Another small miracle, Gabe thought, though not really a miracle because he could've done it without the kid. He could've done it without a boom, too, using the sound on the camera. But it wouldn't have been as good, and Gabe didn't like to skimp on quality.

Finally they were ready to film. While they were setting up, the mother had adjusted her son's cap and her own and put on lipstick. They sat on the edge of the bench, the mom with a worried expression, the kid with a smile. Living in the moment. Reminding Gabe when he'd done that.

Not like now. Now he seemed to be always looking at the next moment.

He asked their first names and why they were at the hospital across the street. He'd pan that in later, he thought, as he listened to their answers, finding out the mother's name was Jen. She told him the basics of Scott's disease. He had a brain tumor in a place impossible to operate on. He'd had radiation to shrink most of it, then his oncologist had put him on chemo to get rid of the rest.

By the time she finished, Gabe was clenching his teeth. Things like this shouldn't happen to kids.

"I hope you'll pay attention." He forced himself to relax as he talked to Scott. "This is important. What's your favorite pie?"

Scott laughed and Jen smiled, some of the tension leaving her shoulders.

"Chocolate with whipped cream," Scott said. "I like pecan and apple, too."

"And banana," Jen said.

"I don't know how I forgot that. I like banana a lot."

"Me, too," Gabe said. "Now, what's the worst part about being sick?"

"Being sick."

Jen nudged his shoulder. "Smart ass."

Scott pointed at the video. "Mom, you swore on camera."

She rolled her eyes, and Scott laughed. Gabe felt his heart squeeze. That's how he'd been as a kid. Laughing even as he knew he was going to die. It was either that or tears that would've made his mom feel bad.

"What else don't you like about being sick?" Gabe asked.

Scott's mouth turned down. "Lots of things. Not feeling good enough to play with my friends. Sometimes not even feeling good enough to talk to them. Seeing my—"

"Seeing what?" Gabe asked.

"Seeing what?" his mom asked.

"You're not going to like it."

Her face tensed, as if she were getting ready for a blow. "Then you need to tell me."

Looking down at his skinny legs, Scott whispered, "Seeing my mom cry."

Tears welled in Jen's eyes. "Oh, Scott." She looked away from him, blinking hard.

There was silence on the camera, which wasn't a good thing, and the minutes were ticking by, but Gabe didn't try to hurry. With only the sounds of traffic and a barking dog in the distance, the pause gave the moment more importance.

When Jen turned back, her eyes were glittering. She bent and kissed her son's thin cheek. "I love you, Scott."

"I love you, too, Mom."

They both looked at Gabe. "What will you do when you're healed?" he asked.

"I'll be nicer to my big sister," Scott said. "And I won't make fun of the other kids that look different."

Jen made a soft exclamation, a mix of surprise, pride and sadness.

"That's laudable," Gabe said, his voice neutral. "What brought that on? Did someone make fun of you?"

"No, but they look at me like I'm an alien." Scott stared into Gabe's eyes. "A lot of them don't want to come too close to me, like they're afraid they'll catch my tumor. And I think it makes them feel bad because they're healthy. They think if it happened to me, maybe it could happen to them. And it scares them."

Jen made another sound, this one mournful.

"What else will you do different?" Gabe asked.

"I don't know what I can do, 'cause I'm just a kid. But when I'm old, I want to be president."

"What will you do as president?"

"I can stop all wars. Wars kill people and cost money. Lots of money. I think instead of spending all the money on a war, we should give the money to the other countries, and maybe they can use it to fix what's wrong. We could make them promise they won't fight anyone or we'll take our money back."

"Brilliant idea."

"I know." Scott nodded his head like a sage.

"We have to go now," Jen said.

"Email me and I'll send you the video," he said. "And the release form."

Jen nodded and stood. "Come on, Scott, we've got to go."

Scott slid off the bench onto his feet. "Will it be on YouTube?"

"Once I get the release form from your mom."

"His older sister would like to see the video," Jen said. "And my mom and dad."

"My teacher would probably show it in class." Scott grinned. "And I thought of something else."

His mom shot him one of the Mom Looks. "Scott, we've got to go."

"Just one minute, Mom." He gazed up at Gabe. "I changed my mind about the pie. I think I'll have peach."

"I'll ask the pie lady to send you a whole peach pie."

"Maybe later," Jen said.

"I can't eat a lot of stuff now. I puke too much. That's another thing I don't like." He waved at Gabe, and the mom and kid hurried away.

Gabe turned to the kid who was helping with the boom to thank him. But the kid was frowning. "I'd like to see that, too," he said.

"Sure. Give me your email."

They put the equipment in his SUV. While the kid wrote his number on the back of one of Gabe's cards, Gabe got out his wallet and handed him a twenty. "Thanks for your help."

The kid looked from the bill to Gabe's face then grinned. "If you need more help, give me a call." He nodded and hurried away, sticking the bill into his back pocket.

Gabe got into his car and looked at the hospital. All the windows with all the patients. And the passion that

had been missing inside him for so long dripped back
like medicine into a dying person's veins.

TWENTY-FOUR

Rosa's oldest son greeted Katie with a kiss on each cheek. His fingers still cupping her upper arms, Matt pulled back, grinned, then leaned forward to plant a kiss on her lips. When Matt released her, Katie laughed. Nothing like a kiss from a good looking young man to brighten a mood.

"You are like sunshine to my morning," he said.

"Have you been practicing that line?"

"I saved it just for you." He glanced down at the box in her hand that had prevented him from full-body contact. "And you brought pie. My day keeps getting better."

"Pie?" Tony, Rosa's second oldest, wandered into the front hall, barefoot with a hunk of hair falling over his left eye, looking as if he'd just rolled out of bed. He was dangerously sexy, or so Katie heard.

She nodded at him, a little cool, disappointed because he continued to work for his dad, though it was none of her business. She turned back to Matt. "I didn't know you were home."

His face darkened, as if a cloud had passed over the house, but the sunny hallway was as bright as a moment ago. "I wanted to talk to my dad."

From the brooding tension in his face, Katie surmised the talk didn't go well. She could have told Matt it was hard to argue with a rectum, but she nodded sympathetically. Pies were much easier than people.

"If I'd known you were coming, I would've made a Welcome Home Pie for you."

"You didn't know?" His left eyebrow rose. "Your spidey-pie sense let you down?"

She smiled. It was good to see Matt again. He'd matured during his time away at the famed culinary school in New York. He looked handsomer, and he seemed more sure of himself, a man who knew where he was going in life.

"I had a Welcome Home Pie, but I already gave it away."

"Trish and Gunner."

"You heard?"

"I stopped off at Wegner's for flowers for Mom. I know all about their return and the quads and Gunner's new job with Earl."

"Taxidermy and upholstery." Tony sneered. "Remember how Gunner acted when he got his journalism degree? He couldn't wait to get out of here."

"They need the money." Matt's tone was decisive, as if that said it all. "They're lucky they can live with Trish's mom until they can afford to move."

Katie sucked her lips in. No mention of Mrs. Brauer's cancer. Linda Wegner didn't know everything.

Rosa hurried into the living room. "Katie! Why are you all standing in the hall?" She lowered her eyebrows and speared each son with her stare. "And why didn't anyone call me?" She switched her gaze to Katie and her pie. "I thought it was one of Matt's friends. What pie did you bring?"

"Blueberry."

"Ah, your thinking pie. You need advice." She stepped forward and grabbed Katie's elbow. "Come into the kitchen. We'll have pie, and we can brainstorm before I go to work."

Though she kept her tone light, her sons' faces clenched with disapproval at the reminder of her job. Too bad, Katie thought. They were sending disapproval to the wrong parent. The injustice made her so mad, she wanted to tell them they didn't deserve pie and couldn't have any.

But if she said that, the one she'd hurt the most would be Rosa, so she turned her back on the two men and followed Rosa through the living room to the rustic dining room next to the open kitchen.

"You can still market the cooking show pilot," Matt said to his mother.

Rosa shrugged, her lips tight. Katie pressed hers together, too. Clearly Rosa hadn't told her sons that she'd sent the pilot to every place she could think of. It was only a little more than two weeks, and maybe months from now, someone might finally look at it and say, "Yes, that's just what I want!" But in the meantime, Rosa wasn't the type to sit at home and fume. Katie doubted she could afford to lounge around the house, either.

"Hey, Katie, your video is cool," Tony said, changing the subject, a middle child thing that made Katie think there'd be hope for him to be a good guy someday despite his father's bad role modeling.

Ducking her head a little, Katie rounded the dining room table. People had been coming up to her with smiles for the last couple weeks, telling her how much they loved her video. It felt odd to be praised for something other than her pies.

"I thought so, too," Matt said. "I showed it to my friends at school. Even a couple of the chefs. They all went a little nuts over what you said about pies. One of the chefs said he was going to show it to all his beginning classes. Tell them if that's not how they felt about cooking, they should pack up their knives and not waste his time."

"So that's why I've been getting so many views." Katie's face was warm. If she weren't carrying the pie, she'd have put her hands to her cheeks.

They reached the kitchen, and Katie put the box on the counter. Tony beat his mother to the box, pulling out the pie while Matt got plates and forks. Rosa, who had trained her boys well, smiled wanly at Katie.

"Gabe was right after all," Rosa said. "People like your short video. It's popular."

Katie shrugged. "The last I checked, the views were about three thousand. That seems a lot to me, but it's really not much."

"I showed it to the woman next to me on the plane," Matt said. "It said your views were at 6900."

"Really?" Katie heard the squeak in her voice. She glanced down at her feet in the sensible sneakers that wanted to do a little happy dance.

"I wonder that I haven't heard from Gabe, crowing about it." Rosa frowned.

Matt narrowed his eyes at her. "That's the videographer, right? Was he bothering you?"

"Not me." Rosa looked at Katie, her eyebrows raised.

Katie gave Matt what she knew must be a weak imitation of Rosa's stare. "I have a father. If I have any problems, I don't need you to help me."

"I hope Sam keeps his shotgun ready."

Tony laughed.

"It's not necessary. Gabe's in Chicago, and I'm here." Katie shrugged, as if it didn't matter.

Matt's expression softened, and Rosa put her hand on

Katie's shoulder. Katie gazed down at her shoes again. Apparently her shrug hadn't fooled them. Who needed a lie detector when you had friends?

"Enough chatter," Rosa said. "Let's eat the thinking pie and brainstorm. I'll get coffee."

"I'll help," Tony said.

"Katie didn't come here for your help, she came for mine," Rosa said.

Matt and Tony looked at Katie. She gestured to include them. "I'm trying to think of a way to help Trish and Gunner." She pushed her hair behind her ear. Tony shoved a plate across the counter at her, a piece of pie and fork on it. "I'm thinking of auctioning off a pie a week. I thought maybe other people in the village will join in to help Trish and Gunner, too."

"Does that pie a week include deliveries?" Rosa asked. "I could do a meal a week, but if the highest bidder is too far from Miracle, I might not be able to deliver."

"Tell Nick to do it," Tony said about Rosa's youngest son.

"Or you could," Matt said.

Tony gave his older brother a look that should've made him explode like a cartoon character. "I'm busier than Nick."

"Yeah, I know what you're busy doing."

"Boys!" Rosa's voice rang out sharply. "This is a thinking pie, not a fighting pie."

"Fighting?" Tony waggled his eyebrows at Rosa. "You see any fists?"

"If there were, I'd win," Matt said.

"Ha! If I weren't eating the pie, we'd see who would win." Tony turned to Rosa. "Not everyone in the village has a talent like you, Mom. Or you, Katie."

"Or me," Matt said.

"You live in New York and won't even be part of this. And when are you going to get it through your inflated head that not everything is about you?"

"This is where my mom lives, so it's definitely about me." Matt gave his brother a male version of his mother's stare. "Just because I'm going to school in New York doesn't mean I don't care about my friends in Miracle. I used to hunt and fish with Gunner. I always liked Trish. I want to help."

"Enough squabbling." Rosa gave both sons The Stare, her lips a dark bluish pink from a bite of pie. "We should sit down and talk about this seriously."

"Some studies show we think better standing than sitting," Matt said.

Tony rolled his eyes.

"Then we'll stand." Rosa turned to Katie. "I know a more efficient way to do this. You're getting so many views, and it's just getting better." She nodded at Matt. "I'm sure it's because you showed so many people."

"Anything to help."

"Hey, I showed my friends, too," Tony said.

"Thank you, too, Tony," Katie said. Despite the serious mission that brought her here, a small happiness hummed through her. "Both of you are wonderful."

They looked at her as if she were their father's special puttanesca sauce and they'd like to eat her, a slow bite at a time. She thought of Gabe and snapped her attention to Rosa, her face warm. She needed him out of her head so she could *think*.

"Before we go any further," Matt said, "are you sure they'll accept the money? I don't know about Gunner. He's proud."

"Gunner's going to be the father of six kids real soon,"

Tony said. "He can't afford to be proud."

"Tony's right," Katie said. "Trish is proud, too. But neither of them is stupid. If they argue, we'll just say they can pay it back some day." Lifting a forkful of pie to her mouth, she looked at Rosa. "What do you mean by an efficient way to do this?"

"What we need to do to raise money," Rosa said, "is get Gabe back to Miracle."

TWENTY-FIVE

Katie choked on her pie. Matt pushed a napkin at her, and Tony rushed to get a glass of water.

She managed to swallow and breathe fast, in and out. Her face, neck and upper chest were hot. She was pretty sure her complexion was a lovely strawberry shade.

Tony handed her a glass of water, his eyebrows raised in a question.

Ignoring his expressive Italian face, she gulped down half the glass then turned to Rosa. This wasn't about her. It wasn't even about Gabe. It was about Trish.

"Why Gabe?"

"If we want a lot of money, it's very simple. We have to go global."

"I think you mean viral," Matt said.

Rosa flapped her hand at him. "Viral, global, whatever. Gabe can film us talking about Trish and Gunner needing help. I'll set up a bank account for the money. People can send us checks, and we'll put it in the bank for them."

"Yeah, right," Tony said, irony heavy in his voice. "We ask for money and people will give it to us. I'm sure that will work as well as when I asked Dad for my last raise."

"Not just *us*." Rosa shot her middle son another scorching look. "The whole village. Maybe we can just tell them how much it matters and even a little about

Miracle."

Both men grimaced, and Katie squeezed Rosa's arm. "It could work. But instead of just putting out a plea for money, maybe we should ask Gabe—or even someone else, because I don't know why he'd do this—"

"He'll do it," Rosa said, in the tone of voice that said *He'll do it after I talk to him.*

"We should ask him to do interviews with other people in the village. Something similar to what he did with me. They can share their story. Then at the end, after they make people care about them, they can say why it's important to do this."

"That's when they ask for money," Matt said. "I like it."

"It could work," Rosa said. "We'll have to make a list of people who have a story." She pushed her empty plate away.

"It's going to be a short list," Tony said.

Katie shook her head. "Everyone has a story."

"Yeah, but we know their stories, and they're boring."

"They're boring to us," Katie said, "but they're not boring to the people who lived it."

"How do you know they're boring?" Matt held out his hands, reinforcing his question. "Who would've thought Katie's story would be interesting? Sorry, Katie."

Tony nodded. "It's true. Sorry, Katie, but you live in your dead grandma's cottage. You hardly date. It's kind of weird to find out you're interesting."

"No offense taken. I'm amazed, too. It's not as if I do anything as interesting as either of you."

They both stared at her for a second, then Rosa laughed.

Matt grinned first. "You're making fun of us, aren't you?"

"You must be the smart male in your family."

"Hey!" Tony said.

Matt snickered then gestured at Katie. "There's a lot of truth in what she said. Maybe everyone's interesting once you find out more about them."

"We think we know our neighbors." Rosa's eyes narrowed and darkened. "Or people close to us. But many times we see what they want us to see."

The grin dropped from Matt's face, and Tony's eyebrows lowered, a brooding, angry look that made Katie wonder how long he would continue to work for his dad. Unlike Matt, she couldn't see him going on to culinary college. Or any college.

"So you agree?" she asked. One crisis at a time. And if Matt and Tony were thinking about helping Trish and Gunner, it would make their own problems seem smaller.

"If you can get this Gabe guy," Matt said, "it's worth a shot. He's got the touch."

Katie's arms prickled. Gabe certainly did have the touch. He didn't just seduce her into telling stories. He seduced her right into bed.

Or did she seduce him? At the time it seemed awfully, wonderfully mutual.

"Sounds good to me," Tony said. "And at the end of the stories, we'll put the information for the website."

"A website?" Rosa frowned. "I wonder if there's a way to do it for free? I could ask Derek Muench. He did the website for our...your father's restaurant."

"I was in the same grade with Derek," Katie said. "I could ask him."

"I was a paying customer." Rosa gave her a determined look. "It's harder to say no to me. I'll ask him."

"Derek will do anything to get away from his mom," Tony said.

"Except move out of her house," Matt replied.

"And they say women are catty," Rosa said. "Elaine has MS. How could he leave her?"

"Hey, we're just sayin' it the way it is." Tony helped himself to another piece of pie. "It's not like she can't get around. When I'm twenty-eight, I don't plan on living with you."

"I can't tell you how grateful that makes me."

Katie felt like she was watching a movie. They even said cutting things to each other with love and humor.

"We'll have to see how we can set this up as a charity." Rosa frowned. "I'll ask my accountant if he can help. This is getting complicated."

"I can ask my dad," Katie said. "He knows people."

"Would you?" Rosa's smile held relief. "I could do it, but Sam would do it better."

"It's better to involve as many people in the village as possible," Matt said. "Make it a community project. Not just yours and Katie's."

Rosa beamed at him. "When did you get so smart?"

"When I moved out of my home," Matt said. "You gotta get smart fast." He snagged a look at Tony.

"Are you talking about me? Hey, I'm only twenty-three."

"So? It's not like you're going to college or school. Why're you still living with Mom? You made fun of Derek, but you're not much better."

"Don't worry about me. I have plans."

"Yeah? What plans?"

"The none-of-your-business kind of plans."

Matt sneered. "That's what I thought you'd say. Maybe this Gabe can get it out of you."

145

"No one's getting it out of me."

"Not even your mother?" Rosa asked.

"See what you started?" Tony glared at his brother, who laughed.

No mercy in that corner, Katie thought.

Tony looked back at his mom. "Sorry, Mom. Hey, I've gotta help prep at work." He put his dessert plate on the counter then headed out the back way, giving them a wave. "See ya later. Let me know how it goes."

"Don't say anything to anyone," Rosa called. "Not until I talk to Gabe. If I find out Linda Wegner knows about this, I'm going to be very angry."

"Mom! *I'm* not the family loudmouth."

"You better not be talking about me," Matt said.

"If the mouth fits..." Tony smirked, then disappeared into the back hall.

"Brat." Matt turned to Katie and Rosa. "Before you do anything, you should consider how much you'll pay this Gabe guy. Don't give him a percent of what the video makes. It's better to pay him a set amount."

"I've been thinking, too." Rosa lifted her eyebrows. "I checked his credentials before I hired him, and he volunteered at one of those world organizations that builds hospitals. He filmed the making of one someplace in Africa and was there for three years. In person he seems cool and a little distant, but maybe he'll do this out of the goodness of his heart." She gestured to Katie. "What do you think?"

Katie blinked at her. "You think he seems cool?"

Matt snickered. Rosa frowned and at him. "Will you be serious?"

"Then stop making me laugh." He dropped his grin. "Mom, maybe it's the right thing to do, but the guy lives in Chicago. You said he does wedding videos. That means he's got rent or mortgage to pay, food to buy. That kind of stuff. A guy like that can't afford to work for free."

"I think you're wrong about the pay. I think he'll come and do it for nothing."

Matt didn't roll his eyes, but to Katie it looked like he wanted to. "Why?"

"Because he wants to sleep with Katie."

Katie stepped back. Her jaw dropped. Did she just hear what she heard? She wanted to say something...anything...but her voice stuck in her throat.

Matt laughed. "So now you're pimping Katie out?"

Rosa reached her hand out to her. "Katie, I didn't mean to say it that way. I—"

Katie snapped around and ran out the front door. She didn't realize until she was outside in the chilly air that she'd left her jacket behind.

Opening the driver's door of her SUV, she remembered her keys and cell phone were in the pockets of her jacket. She groaned and headed back.

Right now she probably needed an Everything Is Going Wrong Pie, but either it would be too bitter to eat or too sugary. No inspiration for it ever came to her.

Some days she just had to settle for plain old apple.

TWENTY-SIX

Sitting across from the hospital administrator, who turned out to be a friend of a friend of a friend of Gabe's stepfather, Gabe kept his smile on, the one he used for the bride and the groom. And, more importantly, the bride's parents.

"I saw your film two years ago on the hospital in Africa," Evonne Black said. She was a fortyish, medium-sized woman, with medium looks, pale skin, and easy to care for short, brown hair. She put her knuckles over her throat. "It was so good, I had to send money, even though the hospital was already built. Very impressive."

He thanked her, and she went on to tell him she'd pass the film he'd done the other day to the hospital's lawyers, that he needed to get written permission from the children's parents or guardians before filming, and there would need to be a parent with him at all times. She requested he email the consent form he'd use for the parents. She'd send that to the lawyers, too.

He nodded with every stipulation. The last didn't make him pause. Good for them for watching out for the kids' safety.

"Though I was impressed with your film credits," the administrator continued, "I have to admit, the video of the pie baker in Wisconsin made me laugh. And the video with the boy made me tear up. I'd like to see this go through. You have a gift."

"I'm mentioning the hospital," Gabe said, standing to hold out his hand, "and can put in a plea for donations for the pediatric wing."

She gave him her hand and put her left hand over his, her eyes bright. "I hope it works out."

He left, his spirits up. As if he'd turned a new corner of his life, and this one was leading to the place where he should be. As if this path had been laid out for him all along, and somewhere he'd taken the wrong turn.

Striding down the hall, he had an urge to call Katie that was so strong he clenched his fingers to keep from taking his phone out of his pocket. Katie was one road; his career was another.

He fought the urge all the way out of the hospital. Taking in a breath of the chilly air coming from Lake Michigan, he finally relaxed his fingers, allowing them to uncurl.

That's when his phone rang. He grabbed it and looked at the caller ID. *Rosa Fabrini.* He stared as it rang again. It wasn't Katie, but he still felt a shot of excitement. Not because of Katie, he told himself. This was professional. The numbers for Katie's video were climbing. He expected to get sponsors soon. Not enough to live on with just one, but if Rosa had changed her mind and he uploaded more videos with two attractive and personable cooks, the hits would multiply and so would the money.

He could do this and the videos for the children. The more product, the more avenues, the more success.

And if he went to Miracle to film Rosa, he would get to see Katie.

He put his cell phone to his ear. "Hello, Rosa. Are you ready to step into the dark side?"

TWENTY-SEVEN

Katie woke up with her nerves tingling.

Rosa had called Gabe four days ago. He was arriving today and would stay for the weekend to film fifty people.

All the while she baked her pies, fed Happy, let her out, packed her pies in the van, and then drove off on her delivery round, her fingertips and toes tingled, the anticipation building.

It was dark when she left home and the sun was beaming when she returned and had an urge to make a pie crust. She thought it was going to be a Welcome Home Pie, but when she grabbed the strawberries and the peaches and the apples, she knew that it wasn't.

She was making the wrong pie, but she kept making it. She didn't tell the pie what to make, the pie told her.

Oh God, this was horrible.

Sitting in Mo's Pub, Gabe felt eyes on him. It was only ten in the morning, and the place was full. On the booths and tables, Gabe saw stacks of onion rings that he guessed must be one of Mo's specialties.

Gabe felt like the main course.

"It's really Katie's idea," Rosa said.

Her words were a punch in Gabe's belly. His mouth opened but his voice caught in his throat.

"She asked me to handle it with you," Rosa continued, watching for his reaction. As if she knew what happened between him and Katie and didn't trust him.

He couldn't blame her. The last time he was in Miracle, he came, he enjoyed and he left.

That's all she knew.

That's all Katie knew.

"So she thought I should come?"

"That was my idea. It was her idea to raise money for Trish and Gunner. We brainstormed with my two oldest sons, and this is what we came up with."

"Oh?" He wondered how old her sons were.

"My oldest is at the Institute of Culinary Education in New York. He's been showing Katie's video to all his school friends and their instructors. They're all impressed."

"Katie's very impressive," he said. Why didn't Rosa just get a hammer and bonk him on the head with it? That would be more subtle. What should he say? That he was sorry he didn't get on his knees and kiss Katie's bare toes?

He stifled a groan. Kissing Katie's bare toes sounded like an excellent idea.

The door opened, and Taz entered the restaurant. Just as when Gabe walked in, everyone turned to stare at him. Though Taz carried his boom pole and his head phones, he looked exotic with his caramel skin and his prowling walk. Like a tiger that escaped from the jungle.

Taz grinned, nodded at a booth of four young women in their late teens, early twenties. The women giggled. He spotted Gabe and strutted toward him.

"Taz is here." Gabe glanced around. "Where are we filming?"

"Mo offered the break room, but I thought his office

would be better."

Apparently Mo had agreed. Rosa was a hard person to say no to.

"Is Katie here?" The question spilled out of him, ignoring the *shut up* message from his mind.

"I called her about ten minutes ago, and she's baking a pie. Why? Do you want her to be here?"

"Just curious. Taz and I are ready to start." Taz reached their table, and Gabe nodded at him.

Rosa gave Gabe a look, as if she saw through him, straight to his soul. He slid out of the booth. Maybe his soul had a few stains, but God owed him a few breaks.

She stood. "Everyone is counting on you. I expect you to do a great job."

"That's comforting," he said, following her. Behind him, Taz laughed.

Gabe felt the curious gazes again as they headed past the bar where a man with several missing teeth beamed at him and a tall, masculine looking woman gave him the once over. Gabe grinned at them. He never liked doing cookie-cutter projects, and this was far from any cookie forms.

He'd taken this job for two reasons: It sounded interesting and he'd get to see Katie again.

For the last reason alone, he would have come. He was doing this for half his usual price, but if Rosa hadn't budged, he would have done it for free just to see Katie.

He suspected he was setting himself up for heartache, but he hadn't been able to stop himself from coming. Before he'd taken the first job for Rosa, she'd told him that some people were addicted to Katie's pies. He suspected he was just addicted to Katie, and one thing he knew about addictions was that they never ended well.

TWENTY-EIGHT

Like a lot of things in Miracle, Mo's back office wasn't what Gabe expected. Gabe thought it would be crowded and small. Instead it ran nearly the width of the back of the bar with a wide window that let in plenty of light. Gabe guessed it had been a living room at one time. Despite the table pushed into a corner, it still looked like a living room. There was an old brown recliner with a crack in the seat and a blue wing chair, with a low table between the two.

Gabe immediately decided on the wing chair. Everyone looked good in blue. Anyone sitting in the brown one would look as if they were settling in to watch a football game on TV.

"Why don't I film you first?" he asked Rosa. They'd talked on the phone once a day for the last four days, and he'd found out more about her. That she was a unique combination of an Italian mom and American mom. That she was a sex bomb and sometimes wasn't afraid to use it. And last, that she had her own ideas on how the film should go.

"I should be last," she said. "Earl Raasch, our village president, is first."

"Anything I should know about him?"

"You want cheat sheets?"

Taz laughed.

"The more I know," Gabe said, "the better questions I

can ask."

"Maybe you'll ask better questions if you don't know the answers."

"Maybe you're right. But maybe I'm right."

She stared at him, the way he'd seen a cat stare at a dog once before it pounced, claws out. But Rosa just shook her head. "You're the first man that ever said that to me. Even my own sons. *Everyone* thinks they're right."

He shrugged. "The world's not black and white."

"I'll second that." Taz raised his hand.

"You're dangerous." Rosa stared at Gabe, ignoring Taz. "You know women too well. How did that happen?"

"I don't know women well." He felt uncomfortable. "I know what matters."

"What does matter?"

"Who's doing the interviewing?"

"Can I interview you at the end?"

He went still. "This isn't about me. This is about Miracle and your friends."

"You just don't want to be interviewed."

"That's right, I don't."

"At least you're honest."

"Lies are like acid. They burn holes in your soul." He glanced at Taz. "I hope you're listening, grasshopper."

"Lies are a part of life. Everyone does them."

"Like women when they tell you you're cute?"

"I'm very cute. Aren't I, Rosa?"

She looked him up and down then shrugged. "If you like cute."

Gabe laughed. "You win. Send Earl in. I'll wing it."

Two minutes later he was checking the lighting on Earl. With his wrinkles and grizzled gray hair, the burly village president needed all the lighting tricks Gabe could think of. The red in his black-and-red flannel shirt matched the color of his nose, not helping Gabe's job any.

Earl plunked his wide butt in the brown chair, saying he used to visit the former owner and always sat in the leather chair. The blue chair was too dainty. A ladies' chair. He said that last with derision.

Gabe checked the lighting and decided nothing would make Earl look good, so he said they were running. Leaning forward, he told Earl to tell the camera who he was.

"I'm Earl Raasch, the owner of Miracle Taxidermy and Reupholstering. I'm also the village board president."

"Why do you think you were voted in as president?"

"No one else wanted it."

Taz laughed.

Earl grinned, his teeth yellow.

"And you did?" Gabe asked.

Earl's bushy eyebrows slanted down, his grin gone. "I've lived in Miracle my whole life. Never married, never had children. But I've got a family." He spread his arms wide. "Everyone in the village is my family. Good or bad." He leaned toward the camera, his brows bristling at it, as if two fuzzy caterpillars were glued to the tops of his eye sockets. "And you better believe, we got 'em both. The good and the bad."

Gabe saw why Rosa listed Earl first. And why she hadn't wanted to explain him. Some people had such big personalities they could only be experienced.

"What do you love?" Gabe asked, expecting something about the village life or, considering Earl's occupation, hunting.

"Life. Myself. God."

"You go to church?"

"I did until the preacher cheated on his wife." His face creased into a satisfied smile, and he nodded. "Guess what? The wife's going to have a baby. And it's not the preacher's."

Taz made a small choking sound and Gabe held back laughter.

"What are you grateful for?"

"That's easy. My mom and my dad. They brought me up to be a good man. Me and my brother Herman who died in Vietnam."

"That must've been tough."

"'Course it was tough. Kids nowadays, they're babies. Always whining about stuff. They don't know yet that life doesn't last forever. You gotta enjoy it while you can."

"What about money?" With every answer, Gabe liked Earl more.

"What about it? I got enough for myself and some in the bank. I can't keep up with all the jobs I get. I just hired Gunner Klumb to help at the business."

"It's because of Gunner that we're doing this. You have anything to say about that?"

Earl stared right at the camera, a spark in his eyes, as confident and commanding as if he'd been speaking in front of cameras his whole life. "Gunner and Trish ain't no freeloaders. They've always worked hard. They have two boys. Trish didn't use any of those baby enhancements to get pregnant. They did it the natural way, and now she's having quads."

Frowning, he stopped talking. Then his face smooshed into a wrinkled smirk. "And that should be a warning to all the boys and girls who do it in cars."

Taz gave another muffled laugh. Earl grinned, then his expression sobered. "It's not funny what's happening to Gunner and his family. He had a good job with good insurance, but after they found out Trish was pregnant with four babies, Gunner got laid off." His face twisted into a scowl. "I don't know if it's a coincidence. Gunner said a bunch of other people got the pink slip the same time, so maybe not. Gunner's paying for his own insurance, and it ain't cheap, no matter what those idiots in Washington say. He tried hard to find another job, but finally they had to come home, broke and without a whole lot of hope."

"So you gave him a job to help him out?"

Earl turned his snarl at Gabe. "I gave him a job 'cause I needed him. Don't think I got a soft heart that I can throw money away." He shifted to the camera again, and this time he wasn't smiling. "Maybe five or ten bucks. I can give that away. If you're watching this, maybe you can, too. If it's too much, don't send anything. But if it isn't, you might want to send what you can, big or little. It will all go to Gunner and Trish. The information will be somewhere, right?"

Gabe nodded.

"He says I'm right." Earl pointed at him, but Gabe kept the camera on Earl as he returned his gaze to the camera. A guy who knew his audience. "Someday it's gonna be your turn to ask someone for something. Sooner or later, it happens to everyone. Send the money, and when you need it, it's going to come back to you." He nodded, his lips pressed tightly and his chin set like a mule's. "And that's the truth."

TWENTY-NINE

"I lived in Manhattan for five years." The middle-aged real estate agent with layered, chestnut hair and discreet makeup carried a hint of city air about her as she gazed into Gabe's camera. "I wanted to be an actress. I waited tables, I bought my clothes at consignment stores. The first year, I used to joke about the small village I came from. The second year, it wasn't funny to me. I missed Miracle so much it was a dagger in my heart."

She stopped to swallow, and Gabe thought it was for effect. Gloria had said she was an actress wannabe. This was the kind of thing they did before continuing.

But she didn't continue, swallowing again. Her face looked suddenly haggard, as if she were staring back at some horrible memory.

He never knew what was going to happen during these interviews.

"But you stayed for another four years," he said.

She nodded, pulling herself together as if aware of the camera, shaking off whatever memory had dragged her into the dark side. Once more an impeccably made up woman in her prime. "My mother was sending me money to supplement my income. She had the only brokerage firm in Miracle. She was a great businesswoman. A great woman all around."

A small smile played upon her face, then she shifted

in the blue wing chair and looked straight into the camera. "I'd been working my way up from waiting tables to walk-ons to small parts, and I'd finally gotten a second lead role in an off-Broadway play. The day it was supposed to open, I got a call from a friend that my mother was sick but didn't want to tell me. I called an airline, then the director to tell him I couldn't make it. I was home that night."

"Your mom...? How was she?"

"She died two weeks and one day later." Tears gleamed in Gloria's eyes. "I was devastated. The village rallied around me. I found out she'd been sick for a year and her friends took her to the hospital, brought her groceries, shoveled her sidewalks, did her laundry..."

Gloria stopped to blink furiously. "I never went back to New York. I heard you were asking what we love..." She swept her left hand out in an encompassing motion. "*This* is what I love. The way we watch over each other. The way the while village watched over my mother. Right now the village is rallying around Trish and Gunner, but there are only 629 of us and we can't do it all. A local farmer gave an acre of land to Trish and Gunner. Nearby businesses donated some of the building materials." She gazed at the camera again. "You can see their names on our website. But they need more. And Trish might have to go to the hospital early and stay there..."

There was another pause while she looked sad, tilting her head so the camera caught her glittering eyes. Gabe mentally applauded as he watched with quiet breaths, waiting to see what she'd do next.

"Aren't we all one global village?" Emotion thickened her voice. "I can speak for a lot of villagers and say we contributed after 911, Katrina, Sandy, and other disasters. I'm not saying that Trish and Gunner's situation is as big as any of that. But doesn't the small stuff count, too? The small towns? The small people?" She smiled with her eyes still glittering. "Whether you contribute or not, God bless all of you."

"That's it," Gabe said. He pushed back from the camera and then he stood and applauded her. Someone else applauded behind him. He turned to see who it was and saw Katie.

He'd expected her, but he hadn't expected the impact, the way this tall woman who looked at him out of vulnerable eyes took his breath away. He hadn't expected the punch in his heart. And he really hadn't expected the lift of his soul, as it said, *This woman. This is the one for you.*

He took one step toward her, and she took one step back.

"Hey, Katie," Taz said. "You're looking good."

"And you look gorgeous. But you know that." She turned to Gloria, her arms out. "You were stupendous!"

Gloria fluffed her hair. "I know." They hugged then Gloria talked about a commercial she did when she was in New York. Gabe stood in place, watching Katie. Not saying anything. Not able to. Still stunned by his reaction to her.

It seemed like moments thumped by before his heart beat slowed and his thoughts regained coherency.

He reminded himself about the kids at the hospital in Chicago and his project there. That was *important.* He needed to do that. No one else could do that as well as he could.

And Katie needed to stay here with her friends and her father and her dog. And most of all, her pies.

He was supposed to be here for a couple days, then he'd be gone. Starting anything again wouldn't be good for either of them.

Then she turned to him. And she smiled.

His breath caught again.

His heart felt the punch again.

She took a step toward him, and he took one toward her, as if a string between them was pulling them together.

He couldn't stop himself, and he knew, deep in the recesses of his sneaky brain, that *this* was the reason he returned to Miracle. For Katie. Even if it were just for a short time, and afterward they'd both be left in a big hurt.

He was going to hell.

But not until after he experienced heaven.

THIRTY

K atie had woken up that morning with the need to make her Happy Pie.

An awful, awful need. She didn't want to be happy because of Gabe.

Making it anyway, she told herself it was because the Miracle Project was going to be a huge success. A lie she didn't believe even as she walked into Mo's and found an empty bar stool. She was relieved to find out Gabe was interviewing Gloria and he'd finished with Earl. She relaxed slightly. If she were lucky, she might not even see Gabe.

She felt a twist in her heart. She'd never been good at lying to herself.

She was sipping coffee and chatting with a former schoolmate when Rosa announced she was next. Katie gave her a startled look and pushed off her stool reluctantly. Rosa hadn't warned her that she'd be interviewed. But it wasn't the worry about being filmed that made Katie's heart thump.

On autopilot, she stood and headed toward Mo's office. Once she slipped inside, her gaze zoomed to Gabe, like Happy smelling food and scampering straight toward it as fast as her arthritic feet could move. Never mind that Happy could hardly see. The nose knew.

Something in Katie knew, too. One glance at him and her heart hammered so loudly she was surprised he didn't hear it. Her skin heated so hot she expected smoke to hiss out of her pores.

She vaguely heard Gloria speaking. Gabe said something and then stood. He clapped and so did the others. Katie clapped, too, doing the *monkey see* thing.

As if in slow motion, he turned and saw her. His eyes widened and darkened, and he took a step toward her. She stepped back, because if she stepped forward it would be a running step. She would be like one of those girls in a TV commercial who ran toward the boy who would catch and twirl her, her legs floating in the air. But with her tall and lanky body, he would probably grunt and fall backward. And drop her. Mustn't forget that.

Taz said something to her about looking good. She replied something silly to him, forcing her lips into a smile. Then she hurried to Gloria to tell her how wonderful she was—though her heart was thundering loudly and everyone in the room but Gabe was wallpaper.

Gloria's two-hundred-watt smile broke through the spell that seemed to have caught her up. Once again Katie told her how good she was, as if Gloria's response to Gabe's questions hadn't been a buzz in her ear, saying "blah, blah, blah."

With great concentration, flexing her brain like a muscle, Katie had a two-minute squeal with Gloria, who said something about New York, her words turning into more "blah, blah, blahs."

It seemed like forever before Gloria squeezed her shoulder and headed to the door, leaving Katie with no choice but to turn to Gabe. As she did a ray of sunshine beamed through the window and illuminated him while he stared at her as if he were starving and she were the only food around.

Just like that, as easy as a breath, her worry evaporated. She smiled. No pretenses. Her defenses melting.

So what if she made a fool out of herself? It wouldn't be the first time. Not even the hundredth time.

He smiled back, as if he was ready to make a fool out of himself, too. They'd be two fools together.

Gazing into his eyes, she stepped toward him and he stepped toward her.

He took her hands and smiled at her. Her heartbeat slowed, her skin turned to normal and her brain seemed to be in control again. As if she'd been spinning out of control and his grip stopped her freefall and the brains rattling inside her head. As if their clasped hands turned wrong into right.

This is the way it's supposed to be. Then the hurt came, because *supposed to be* was *never going to be.* Yet she still smiled at him. Just for today, she would live for the moment.

"It's your turn," he said.

"If you say so," she replied and immediately felt like one of those dippy girls who did whatever the male told her to do. She pulled her hands from his and stepped back, keeping the smile on her face. "Rosa said so, anyway, and once she makes up her mind, it's like talking to Happy."

"I thought your Beagle couldn't hear," Taz said.

"Exactly." She headed to the blue chair and sat. She wore a skirt that came just above her knees, but as she sat on the blue chair and crossed her legs, it rose up her thigh. Gabe and Taz's gazes went straight to her legs.

Feeling warm again, she uncrossed them and set her feet in her bargain store black shoes firmly on the wooden floor.

Gabe grinned at her. So did Taz. Katie wished Rosa was in the room to stare sternly at them.

"Say something," Taz said.

"Okay." She remembered his sound tests. "Should I talk about Trish and Gunner?"

"Tell us about your skirt," Gabe said.

"My skirt?" She laughed. "It's my church skirt."

"You go to church often?"

She shook her head. "Only with friends on special occasions. My dad only goes to church on weddings or funerals. My grandmother was pretty much the same way."

"Your family doesn't believe in God?"

"Sure. Well, Gram did. My dad believes there's something out there. Some higher power that has the secret to everything and leaks it out a little at a time. On a need-to-know basis."

Taz laughed, and she relaxed. It was like being back in her kitchen with her pies and the awareness of Gabe thrumming through her. "He likes to say you don't even have to be good to catch the secrets. You just have to be paying attention."

"Did you ever catch it?"

"Maybe. My dad said he tastes the higher power in my pies."

"Amen," Taz said.

"You have a great dad," Gabe said.

"Sometimes I think how lucky I am, and it fills me up." She pressed her hand over her breastbone. "I have a great dad, a great dog, great friends. And I make pies for a living. I'm blessed. That's why I want to do this for Trish and Gunner. I think if you are as blessed as I am, you need to share it or it will go away."

"I know a lot of nasty rich people," Taz said, "and

their money just seems to multiply."

"In this life it multiplies." She scrunched her face. "You don't want to know what's going to happen to them in the next go-round."

Both men laughed, and she grinned. "When are we going to start?" she asked.

"You just did," Gabe said, then he and Taz laughed again at her dropped jaw.

She clamped her mouth shut. "That's not funny. You can start asking me questions now."

"Yes, ma'am." Gabe nodded at her. "Tell us who you are and what you do."

"I'm Katie Guthrie," she said, glad that he wasn't using what she said already, "and I make pies for a living."

"I understand this was your idea."

She was shaking her head before he finished. "Rosa is the evil genius behind this. It was my idea to raffle off pies, and I thought other villagers might join me to help Trish and Gunner. I went to Rosa first. She thought of doing the videos, then she ran with it."

"Do you think it's a good idea?"

"Yes. The whole village is excited and happy to help our friends. This is a big thing."

"A miracle was prophesied last spring. Do you think this fundraiser is the miracle?"

"I think this is something people should be willing to do for each other."

"Do you believe in miracles?"

She looked him in his eyes, and for a second, it felt as if it were just him and her. No Taz, no camera, no boom. Just him, just her. Rays of light circling them, so bright they blocked off anyone else.

"Yes. And I believe in angels, too."

He stared at her for a long moment, dead silence in the room. "That's it," he said finally.

Taz pulled the boom away from above her. She got up silently then ran her hands down her hips and upper thighs, smoothing wrinkles from her skirt. Then she nodded and walked out, feeling their gazes on her, the air charged with electricity.

THIRTY-ONE

Katie left but the current stayed, humming through Gabe for the rest of the day. He and Taz shortened the process but only finished twenty interviews before they stopped at four o'clock. The last subject was an attractive college student who'd come home for the day to do this because Trish had been her babysitter when she was young. She said she loved Trish and wanted the best for her. When Gabe asked her what else she loved, she said, "Coldplay."

Immediately Taz said, "Me, too!"

Apparently the appreciation for the same band had formed an instant bond, as she and Taz left with their arms wrapped around each other's waists.

Taking longer to pack up, Gabe wondered what band Katie liked. What music she listened to in the early morning as she made her pies. Did she hum along? Her hips swaying? Or—

Footsteps on the wooden floor brought his eyes to Rosa. She wore a red top and black slacks, and probably every man who came into Mo's to eat tonight, from thirteen to ninety, would check her out before the menu. She had the old-time stripper figure that even gay men appreciated.

Katie didn't have that. She had something else that Gabe couldn't define. Something that pulled him to her as if she were a giant magnet and he a small nail.

"Everyone came out of your interview smiling." Rosa bestowed upon him an approving nod. "You're good."

"I try."

"You don't try, you *do*. I know you said the first fifty, but I'd like to—"

"No."

She put her hands on her hips. "You're not listening to what I have to say."

"If you want me to do more than fifty, you'll have to pay me more."

"This is for charity."

"I'm charging half my usual rate."

"Someone else might have done it for free."

"Then you should've asked someone else."

"Trish and Gunner need help *now*. I don't have time to vet filmmakers."

He shrugged. "I'm here. I'm good. You're lucky to have me."

She narrowed her eyes at him. "What if Katie agreed to go out with you? Would that change your mind?"

He stilled. "Exactly what are you suggesting?"

"I said *out* with you. Nothing more." She put a hand to the side of her head, pushing up her dark hair. "Why does everyone think I'm pimping out Katie?"

"Listen to what you say." He packed up the rest of his equipment. "You have thirty more appointments. If someone is important, you can stick them in there."

"You were much nicer the last time you were here."

Looking at the frustration on her face, he shook his head. "You're a crazy woman."

"I don't think I'm asking too much."

"Five extra interviews. That's it."

"Ten."

He picked up his lighting and camera equipment.

"Five or none."

Her nostrils pinched and her jaw set. "Okay, five." She turned to leave.

"Don't forget to say thank you."

With a laugh, she glanced back at him. "Have dinner here. It's on me. Be here in an hour."

He watched her leave and wondered what she was planning.

"Come to Mo's for dinner tonight at six," Rosa said.

"I have leftovers." Katie looked at the pecan-apple pie on the counter. Her Happy Pie. There had been moments of happiness during the day. A breathless delight when she was interviewed by Gabe. The sense of being 100% alive, with all her cells sparking, her emotions dancing.

But now she was home and that flush of emotion had washed away, leaving her feeling like a kid after a ride on the giant roller coaster, sad because none of the other rides would be half as thrilling.

"I talked Mo into putting my lasagna on his menu," Rosa said. "All those years we had to eat Mike's old-fashioned lasagna. Mine is healthier and better. It has squash and spinach, and you will die for it."

"I don't want to die."

"Then you'll live for it. You'll want to eat it every day for a week. After that, you'll just want to eat it one day a week."

"Another time I'd love to come, but I've been up since three this morning. I have a good book to read, and I'll probably go to bed early."

"I need you. Not enough people are ordering my lasagna. They read *squash* and *spinach* and think it's health food. No one in Miracle wants to eat health food.

You can eat my lasagna and tell everyone how good it is."

"Why not have your boys do it?"

"They're my sons. People won't believe them. I have a surprise guest coming, too. You won't want to miss this guest."

"You're not going to tell me who it is, are you?"

"Nope."

"It's not Gabe, is it?"

"I'm not a matchmaker, if that's what you're thinking. You should know that right now I'm not a fan of any matches."

"Okay, I'm sorry for my suspicions." And a little sorry it wasn't Gabe, she admitted to herself. "I'll come. I'll eat. I'll enjoy. I'll rave. I'll talk to your surprise guest." Trish, Katie thought. It would feel like old times sitting across a table from Trish and talking about anything and everything. "Will that make you happy?"

"Be there at six. I'll reserve a table in your name." Rosa hung up.

Katie stood, still holding the phone. When the phone rang, she'd half expected to hear Gabe on the other end. After all, he was the reason she'd baked her Happy Pie.

She could call him. He would come. She knew it.

But in the end it would be a booty call.

She set down the phone. It wasn't sex she wanted from Gabe. It was to gaze into his blue eyes and see them sparkle at her.

It was to admire his smile with the dimple lines.

It was to just breathe the same air as him. To talk to him with that electricity zigzagging between them, as if Thor was in heaven, looking down at them and throwing thunderbolts.

With a shiver she crossed her arms. Her kitchen had always been her calm center. Her safe place. But lately she never knew what might happen anywhere. Even here.

It could be something wonderful...or something terrible.

Right now, both choices scared her.

Needing to move, to do *something*, she turned to her pantry and pulled out the flour, sugar, vanilla, cinnamon. Then she crossed to the refrigerator and pulled out butter and cream. She slid open the overlarge fruit drawer. And just stared into it. For the first time in her life, not knowing what pie to make.

THIRTY-TWO

Gabe had expected Mo's Place to be nearly empty, people relieved to be back in their comfortable and quiet homes. Instead it was crowded, the noise level high with punctuations of laughter. The air shimmered with expectation.

Gabe suspected they were waiting for their miracle.

Good luck to them. He'd had his miracle at a young age and wasn't expecting to get struck with a miracle twice. For tonight, he only expected a good meal.

He swept his gaze around the room, searching for Rosa. Past the bar area with the booths on the sides and in front of the long window then into the dining area—

His gaze stopped.

His heart stopped.

One beat. The next beat his heart thumped to life. Stronger than before. Energy pumped into it. Pumped into every cell of his body.

In the far corner Katie sat at a table for two. He strode toward her. Someone called his name. He nodded, waved and kept walking.

As if she felt his intensity, she looked up and her mouth opened in an O. And her face...it softened the way a mother's did when her child walked in. The way a child's did, spotting a puppy.

He sat across from her. He wasn't her puppy, but he wouldn't mind being her man.

While he was here.

The thought saddened him, and her eyebrows indented in a slight frown. "Rosa said she had a surprise guest coming and our dinner was on her. She told me it wasn't you. I thought it was going to be Trish."

"Disappointed?"

Her forehead smoothed and she shook her head. "I don't disappoint easy."

He nodded. It made sense. When someone lived the first five years of their life with an addict who liked you best when you hardly spoke, it didn't give you high expectations of life.

No wonder she lived in her dead grandmother's house and was content to make pies. No wonder she was content with her dog, her father and her friends. Miracle was her safe place. A place that allowed her to thrive.

"What about you?" she asked.

It took him a second to remember he'd asked if she was disappointed. Her hand was on the table, and he covered it with his.

She glanced up, her eyes startled. "By the end of the night, nearly everyone in Miracle will be talking about this."

"Everyone?"

"Pretty much."

"Including your dad?"

Her lips twisted in a smile. "Oh, he'll know."

He smiled back. As if this were a game. And it was. A very old game. "Does he have a shotgun?"

"This is hunting country. In Miracle, shotguns and rifles are part of the male rite of passage. Though quite a few women hunt, too." She leaned toward him, and he leaned toward her. "But he won't use it on you."

"Good to know."

"I hoped it would be."

Her smile widened, and it was like the sun shining from her to him. Tension slowly eased out of his tightened muscles like toxins leaking out of a room.

Rosa stopped in front of them. He hadn't noticed her coming. "Dinner's on me," she said.

"Lobster?" Sitting back, he lifted an eyebrow.

"Go out and catch one. I'll throw it in a pot for you myself."

"Are you matchmaking?" he asked.

Katie pulled her hand from beneath his. He slid his back to his end of the table. Not out of the game yet.

"I'm not a big believer in making matches." Rosa shrugged, her breasts following the movements of her shoulders.

"What do you believe in?" Katie asked.

Rosa squeezed Katie's shoulder. "I believe that you're my good friend, and I want to see you stretch beyond your safety zone, even if it's just for a couple days." She pitched her voice low, so only the two of them could hear her. "You don't want to be my age and have regrets. You don't want to be *any* age with regrets. I see the need in your eyes—" She glanced at Gabe and back to Katie. "In both your eyes. If you don't take advantage of this small pleasure, I have the feeling you'll be sorry."

Katie's gaze shifted to him. In her eyes he saw confusion and darkness. She blinked then looked back to Rosa.

"There's more to life than what goes on in your kitchen," Rosa said in the same low tone. Then she straightened and turned to Gabe. "You like Italian?"

Right now, Gabe loved Italian. He put his right thumb and first two fingers to his mouth and kissed them. Rosa laughed. "I'll make your dinner choice. You'll love it."

She snapped around and hurried away.

"So this was a set-up," he said.

Katie nodded, not saying anything, just staring at him, as if she were considering everything Rosa said.

"I don't know about you, but Rosa nailed me." He didn't take his stare from Katie's face. Her eyes blinked and her mouth parted, as if for a kiss. "When you left today, it felt like a piece of me went with you."

Her eyebrows went up, her eyes widened.

He frowned. Until he said the words, he hadn't realized how badly he wanted her. "I'm probably scaring the hell out of you. You can leave. Don't worry, I won't stalk you."

"I have a question first."

"What?"

"Your motel room or my house?"

THIRTY-THREE

Gabe smiled so widely he thought anyone looking at him would know how he felt. "Anywhere you say. I feel combustible."

"And I'm melting." Katie smiled back at him, a come-to-bed smile.

"Melting like the Wicked Witch of the West?" he asked.

"Idiot. I'm melting like the richest, most revered, most expensive chocolate. Slowly and delectably."

He stifled a groan. She was killing him. "If you were a pie right now, what would you be called?"

"That's easy. Sex." She looked up at the waitress stopping by their table. "But here's our food first."

He nodded. First fill the hunger in their bellies. Then they'd fill the big one that started in their senses, in their brains. That made everything sharper, more exciting, with promises in the air and in their eyes while their skin prickled and their heart thundered. And then that excitement and promise sizzled downward.

He grabbed his fork to dig into his food. When you were offered something wonderful, you wanted to grab it, taste it, touch it and enjoy every second before it ended.

Maybe they couldn't make a beautiful life together, but they would damn well make beautiful memories.

Inside Katie's back hall, she knelt and hugged the Beagle greeting her and Gabe. Her heart was so full of expectations, it was amazing she hadn't danced around Mo's entire restaurant and bar area, hugging and kissing everyone. She'd only refrained because then they would know.

Some things she didn't want the whole village to know. From the gazes she'd felt as she left, she knew they guessed. But at least she hadn't jumped on the bar and shouted, "I love this man!"

After she let Happy out, Gabe said, "She must hear something."

"Because she was waiting?" Katie hung up their jackets, thinking it wouldn't be long before their clothes followed. "I've read studies about dogs who knew their special person was coming home even though it wasn't their normal time. Even when their people were miles away. Dogs must have a sixth sense."

"They're connected the way we're connected."

"I know." Her voice was breathy as she led the way into the kitchen. That's why she'd made the Happy Pie this morning. The pies talked to her first. The man second.

That was one thing she was keeping to herself. No man liked being second to a pie.

Before she finished the thought, he scooped her up and put her on the end of the cooking island. "This is where the magic happens, isn't it?"

Her breath caught in her lungs, stopping her words. She nodded and gave a long exhale. She was melting again. Melting with desire.

A howl came. Then another. "Don't move," he said. "I'll get it."

As she listened to him let Happy in, the expectant

feeling inside her grew. As if it were Christmas, and she was going to get the best gift ever.

A few seconds later, he stalked toward Katie. Like a tiger stalking its mate, she thought, and stifled a giggle.

"Where were we?" he asked, in front of her now.

"You tell me." Her voice sounded odd. Thickened. Her body felt odd, too. Like molten gold.

He put his hands on the counter, one on each side of her thighs, and leaned forward. As his face neared hers, she kept her eyes open, gazing into his eyes and thinking they were the color of heaven.

Then his lips met hers, and her eyes closed slowly, as slowly as the kiss. A soft kiss. A sigh of a kiss. After a moment, she raised her hands to each of his cheeks, a slight stubble tickling the heels of her palms.

Slanting her face, she kissed him harder, taking control. A sound came from deep in his throat. A primal call. She wrapped her legs around his hips, crossing her ankles behind him, her body answering the need in his voice.

He growled again, and a softer imitation of it came from her.

He pulled away. His face was flushed with color. His eyes glittered. "I wanted to do this slowly."

"We can go slow next time."

"On the counter?"

"We can. I'd have to bleach it afterward."

With a laugh, he released her and stepped back. She smiled, though it hadn't been a joke. She would have bleached the counter.

She pushed off to stand on the floor, then took his hand and led him out of the kitchen and up the stairs to her bedroom. He was quiet behind her, a hush loud with rising desires.

When they reached the bedroom they started pulling off their clothes, both at the same time. Wordless. The passion taking over her. A tiny corner of her brain marveled and celebrated. It seemed with their clothes they were stripping off all that was extraneous. Nothing mattered more than the two of them joining together.

"I'm glad you brought protection." She slipped out of her panties, losing the race to get rid of her clothes and be the first one naked.

He looked up at her, his expression serious. "I don't know if I am."

Her breath sucked in. Then he was ready for her, and God knew she was ready for him. She'd been ready since she walked into Mo's office this morning. If she'd had to wait one more second, she probably would have jumped him, saying, *"Now! Do it now."*

They tumbled onto the bed, and he was doing *it* to her. Doing it wonderfully. Kissing, touching, squeezing. And she was kissing, touching, squeezing right back.

He pushed inside her, and she was wet, so wet. A noise came out of him, another primal sound shuddering through her.

"You're so damn good," he said, his voice hoarse.

She hadn't done anything except respond to the sexiest man she'd known. Before she could tell him, he was moving inside her, rubbing against *that* spot, that wonderful spot that sent tremors through her. Strangled screams came from her mouth and she gazed up at him. His head was back, a look of agony on his face as if he were in pain.

Or in ecstasy.

Again. And again. And again.

Then it came. A big one. Rapture shattering through her. She felt as if she stood on the top of the world and could see its wonders all around her and none of the ugliness.

But only the two of them were in this world, holding onto each other, shuddering in each other's arms. As if an earthquake had taken place, the world splitting, for a second time the most beautiful thing she'd experienced.

He shuddered on top of her, and it took a moment for her to relax, feeling boneless, her breathing slowed. He rolled off her, and the air was cool against her chest.

"Thank you," he said.

"My pleasure."

He laughed, and so did she. They sounded so polite, as if she were a clerk at a store who had helped him with a transaction. She told him to use the bathroom first. As soon as he left the bedroom, she closed her eyes, a happy sleepiness hovering above her.

He returned to the room and it was her turn. The tiles in the bathroom were cold on her soles as she looked at her face in the mirror and saw she'd been walking around with a smile. When she padded back to the bedroom, her whole body felt like one big smile. She paused just inside the doorway. Gabe was half dressed, sitting on the foot of the bed, his left leg crossed over his right knee, his shoe in his hand, ready to put it on.

He glanced up at her. Unlike him she wasn't wearing a stitch of clothes. His hands holding the shoe froze; his eyes moved up and down, taking in the sight of her naked body. Every curve there for him to see. Every flaw.

She stood tall, letting him look his fill. His gaze warmed her, and her body thrummed, the hunger reawakened. The desire to have him again.

Watching the stillness of his body, the way he looked at her as if he wanted to eat her, she wanted him so badly that this feeling was too much, too big, too brilliant.

"Would you like...pie?"

"Later I'd like pie."

Aware of his gaze still on her, she headed to the closet for the silk robe an old boyfriend gave her for Christmas long ago that she had never worn. Until now.

"Sex is a lot like eating pie." The robe slithered around her, and her skin was so sensitive tonight, it heightened her sensuality. "Sometimes you have to have it right away. Sometimes waiting for it makes you appreciate it all the more."

He laughed low in his throat and she heard the bed creak as he stood. She finished tying the sash and looked up. He had pulled on his T-shirt, and was snapping his jeans closed.

She led the way down the stairs and into the kitchen, smiling, feeling...happy. Like her Happy Pie.

As they stepped into her bedroom again, she wondered what pie she would make tomorrow.

THIRTY-FOUR

When Katie returned after her morning pie run, the sun was just coming up and Gabe's car was still in the driveway. A hum started in her throat.

Happy waited for her at the door as usual. She bent to hug Happy—she wanted to hug everyone today—before letting Happy scamper out like she was a puppy.

She headed to her bedroom and peeked inside. Gabe was sleeping, the covers pushed below his ribcage, his legs spread beneath the covers with one arm out to her side of the bed, as if reaching for her. Rays of sunlight streamed through the window and formed a nimbus around his face, shoulders and upper body.

She was backing away when a trill came. She hesitated and it came again. Spotting the source of the noise, she stepped inside, grabbed his jeans and crossed to Gabe. She shook his shoulder, his skin warm under her palm.

His eyes opened, staring up at her. A smile stretched his lips, and she started to smile back when another trill came from the phone.

"Your pants are ringing." She dumped the pants on his chest then snapped around to leave.

"'Morning to you, too," he said, laughter in his voice.

A howl came from outside the back door, and she hurried to let the dog in. She petted Happy then turned to the sink to wash her hands. As the warm water streamed over her hands, the need started. Not for sex this time, not for Sam. For pie. To her, this need was as primal as sex. When it called her, she answered.

She pulled the ingredients out of the cupboards and refrigerator. The usual suspects first: sugar, flour, salt, eggs, vanilla. Then sour cream, cream cheese, pineapple, walnuts...

The name of the pie hit her, and she dropped the half-filled bag of walnuts. The clip holding the bag shut popped off and walnuts scattered out, flying across the floor.

A snuffle came from Happy's corner, then dog feet tapped on the tile. Katie still stood there, unable to move as Happy stopped, finding a walnut, then another and another. Like a catfish on the bottom of the aquarium, gobbling up the food the other fish missed. The bottom feeders.

Slowly, as Happy neared the bag with walnuts still in it, Katie bent and picked it up. She felt as if she'd aged fifty years, cold from the inside out.

She was putting the bag away when she heard heavy footsteps from the bedroom. Gabe had put his shoes on, which told her he wasn't staying for another round of lovemaking.

No surprise. The pie had already told her what to expect.

She knelt on the floor to find any walnuts Happy might have missed. Happy didn't eat as fast as she used to though she gave it the old Beagle try.

"What happened?" Gabe's black leather shoes stopped a foot from her hand.

"I dropped the walnuts." She kept gathering walnuts, not looking up. When she finished, she crossed to

Happy's food bowl and spilled the walnuts into it. Happy wouldn't complain about a little floor dirt.

"Does this happen often?"

"No." She faced him. "You're leaving?"

He backed up, not replying right away.

Suddenly breathing was hard for Katie. She forced herself to suck air into her lungs, forced her lungs to expand and then contract, to allow her to breathe in and then out.

"Not until after I'm done filming today," he said.

She nodded. Her emotions were numb now, and she liked it that way.

"I have to work when I get home," he added.

"Of course you do." She smiled as if it didn't bother her.

"It's important." He lowered his gaze. "Important to me."

"Of course."

He made a sound of frustration. "Not because it's a job. It *means* something."

"You don't have to explain anything to me."

"I want to. I'm filming interviews with children who have cancer. The format's similar to the one I did with you. To what I did yesterday. I spoke to the hospital administrator before I heard from Rosa. It's the same hospital I was in as a kid. A PR assistant just called to give me the go-ahead. She'll help me facilitate the interviews, but I have to find the children myself and get permission from the parents."

He watched her intently, his gaze dark and serious. A turnaround from the cool, laughing guy she'd met, just a few weeks ago when the leaves on the trees were the brightest he'd seen.

Now the leaves were rotting on the ground.

"This feels like a second chance for me," he said.

"Second chance for what?"

"To do something that matters."

She raised her eyebrows. Sending a silent question.

"I was a fool when I went to Africa." He raked his fingers through his hair, his eyebrows down, his forehead furrowed. "I expected everyone to be happy to help out. Instead everyone had their own agenda. Even Mother Nature. By the time it was over, I just wanted to get home and not do anything for anyone. I was wiped out, emotionally numb. Ever since then, I've skated through life. Lived it without passion. Do you know what that's like?" He grimaced. "Of course you don't. You have your pies."

"I know my pies aren't as important as your videos, but—"

His shaking head stopped her. "I'm not mocking you. When I first met you, I envied you. Now I've found something that fulfills me. Something that clicks here." He thumped his fist over his heart. "Only I'm getting double clicks, because you click in my heart, too."

"Is that what we were doing?" Her heart was crying. "Clicking?"

He gave her a smile filled with sadness. "For years I've been avoiding anyone who made me feel deeply. And then I met you."

"Of all the pie joints," she said, "in all the villages in all the world, he walks into mine."

He laughed abruptly, but there was no laughter in his eyes.

There was no laughter in her heart, either.

"It's all right." She raised her hands to the sides of his face. Staring into his eyes, she memorized the color, the way they looked at her as if she were precious. "I'm okay.

I'm not going to fall apart. You have to do this, and I understand."

"I should have told you last night."

"Stop." She let go of him and stepped back. "Just shut up. I'm glad we had last night, and if you're sorry about it, then I will get pissed."

"If you knew how much I wanted to stay..." He frowned. "I just can't do what I want here."

"I get it. This is a small village and you want to do big things." She held herself tightly. If she didn't, she'd start trembling. It was hard to keep looking at him, knowing he was going to leave. She just wanted him to go. If he stayed much longer, she'd do something stupid—like cry in front of him.

He looked away from her. "You were making a special pie? What kind?"

"The kind I normally bring to people in mourning or depressed."

"Someone you know is in mourning?"

Her shoulders tensed and she shrugged. "I had an urge to make it."

"What's your name for this pie? Mourning Pie?"

She shook her head. "Sad Pie."

He looked at her for a long moment. She looked back and wished he'd leave. He had to go on with his life. Fine. It was just one night. She'd get over it. She had an angel fixation, but he was no angel. As far as she knew, angels didn't do what they'd done last night in her bedroom.

"What are you thinking?" he asked.

"I was thinking that for an angel, you make love pretty damn well."

He laughed, his head back. She wanted to laugh with him, but couldn't. Afraid it would turn into tears when there was no reason to cry.

"You should go," she said. "Finish this job and leave."

Still he remained standing in front of her. Frowning now and looking down, his eyes blank, not seeing her, just seeing something in his mind that he didn't like much.

Then he blinked and the blankness in his eyes was gone. This time when he looked at her, she could tell he saw her.

"I can't stay," he said slowly, "but you could come to Chicago."

THIRTY-FIVE

S he looked shocked, as if he'd suggested she take a pastry knife and stab herself in her heart. "I have customers. People count on me."

"Sure, I understand." He always understood. But that didn't stop him from wanting it to be different. "I'd better go."

Her forehead crinkled, but she nodded. He took one glance around at this place that had become so familiar to him. She called him her angel, but she'd been the angel for him. She'd been his inspiration for the video. Her reminders of his leukemia had been the impetus that sent him to the hospital where he had the idea for the videos with cancer kids. Something that mattered.

"I understand you came back because of the videos for Trish and Gunner," she said, "but there's not likely to be another video. I guess this is goodbye."

He looked at her, and a big sadness crashed down on him. Sunlight shone brightly in her kitchen but inside him was darkness.

"I didn't come because of the job. It was an excuse. I came because of you."

Her eyes widened. "You didn't call."

"You didn't call me, either. I should've stayed in Chicago, lining up kids to interview. Helping your friends is a good cause, but it's not my cause. I could've given you the names of other filmmakers who would've done as good of a job as I did."

"I don't believe that. You're the best."

The darkness thinned, letting light in. "I won't kiss you. If I do…"

"Yeah." Her eyes were shadowed, her lips curved down.

Nodding, he turned to leave. He had two voices in his head. One told him to leave and do the work he loved. Another told him to stay with the woman he might love.

Both voices were loud. Both voices were adamant.

He started for the door.

Behind him, she said, "I'll call you."

He froze then looked over his shoulder at her. "If you call, it's going to make it harder to get on with my life."

She shrugged. "Who said it was supposed to be easy?"

He walked out, forcing his feet to move, though they felt as if they weighed a ton. As if his shoes had turned into cement.

And his chest felt funny. Different from when he'd walked inside yesterday, so hopeful and so horny.

When he turned his SUV onto the road leading toward Mo's, he realized what the problem was. He was driving away without a piece of his heart. He'd left that behind him.

THIRTY-SIX

At 5:43 PM Happy stood in the kitchen, her jaws raised, her ears flapping back, and howled. Katie dropped the handful of silverware she had just taken out of the dishwasher. They clattered on the floor. She didn't look down. Instead she stared at her dog who howled again, the sound mournful.

Gabe. He must have left the village. Somehow Happy knew.

A shiver went through her and she felt sick. The phone rang and she stepped over the silverware to it. Feeling like a zombie, she looked at the name on the display. Linda Wegner. Of course. Linda wanted to be the first to tell her Gabe had left. She wanted to be the first to hear Katie's reaction.

Katie wanted to tell her that her old Beagle already told her, but then Linda would call everyone in the village and tell them that she always knew Katie was crazy, but now she had proof.

Linda Wegner was the paparazzi of Miracle.

Katie let it ring and went outside. It was getting dark already, but there was a light on in the barn Sam mostly used for his farm equipment.

When she entered, her shoes scuffing on the ground, he was leaning over his tractor. He straightened. "Hey, sweetheart."

Tears threatened but she smiled instead. "Hey, Dad.

Guess what I almost baked?"

"Knowing you, it could be anything and it would be delicious."

"My Sad Pie."

His eyebrows whipped up. "Sad? Anyone dying?"

Just my heart, she thought. "Gabe's gone. Back to Chicago."

"I see." He grabbed a rag to wipe oil from his hands. "I saw his car by your place this morning. You want him?"

She nodded. "He wants me, too."

"But he left."

"He's making videos in Chicago. Interviewing kids with cancer." She grimaced to hold back an onslaught of tears. "He's not coming back. His dreams are big, our village is small."

"You can do big things in a small village." He gestured, the ends of the rag flapping. "Look what we did this weekend. Your guy put up a few videos on YouTube already. Rachel said money is dribbling into the PayPal account she set up. Not much yet, but when all the videos are up and more people watch them and tell their friends, the money will come."

"He's not my guy."

"You'd like him to be. You wish he was."

"I don't expect every wish of mine to come true."

Sam frowned. "How could he not love you?"

"I don't know. It's amazing how many men don't."

His gesture told her what he thought of the men she'd dated before this. "They weren't the right ones. You feel he's the right one?" He lowered his head. He looked like an old hippie with his long white-streaked hair tied in a tail at his nape and the left knee of his jeans ripped. His lean face and body had seen some years and some tears, along with love and laughter.

She nodded. "He's so right for me that it scares me."

He gave her a long look, and she turned to gaze outside the open barn doors at the fields with the crops cut down. That's how she felt sometimes. Like she was cut down, tamed. For her own good.

When that feeling hit her, she usually hit the kitchen and made pies. Her way of running from life. Her way of coping.

"This is because of your mom, isn't it?" Sam asked.

She whipped her gaze back to him. He scowled, looking angry and sad at the same time. And she cringed, seeing that he wasn't done yet.

"Because she dropped you off at the farm when you were five."

"Like an unwanted package," she said with a smile and a shrug, making a joke about it.

But he wasn't laughing. And neither was she. She curled her hands to keep from grabbing the shovel leaning against the barn wall then hitting the wall with it.

Where had this anger come from? Had it been there all these years?

"She couldn't help it, honey."

"The hell she couldn't." The anger roared up and she yelled the words at him. Flung them like they were weapons. Which was ridiculous because she didn't yell, she didn't fling, she didn't grab shovels to knock holes in barn walls.

"She was an addict."

"She's recovered and remarried. I never met my half sisters. She never invited me."

"Sweetie, there's a reason for that."

"What?"

"She's a selfish bitch."

Katie stared at him, and he looked back at her with tenderness and love and total acceptance. The opposite of her mother who sent her cards that talked about love and acceptance, but she didn't mean any of it.

With a hoarse cry, Katie hurled herself at Sam. He slung his arms around her and held her as tears ran down her face. Along with the sadness and the anger and the hurt, she felt gratefulness and total love.

That's what Sam gave her. That's what her gram had given her. All these years she'd been telling herself and other people how lucky she was. It was a story she made up. Other people believed her, and she'd thought she believed it, too.

Today, she finally did. She was so lucky. She was the luckiest woman in Miracle.

She raised her head and sniffed. "You're the best dad in the world."

"And you're the best daughter." He put his hand on the top of her head, and it felt like a benediction. "Don't be afraid of life."

"The thing is, I don't know if I am afraid." She stepped back from him, giving her a better view of his face. "I have a great life."

"In Miracle," he said.

"It's home." She wiped moisture from beneath her eyes. "Not because of anything to do with my mom. It's Happy. And it's my cottage that makes me think about Gram. Sometimes I can feel her smiling down on me, sending me love. And it's all my customers. It's experiencing the four seasons, even when I complain about the heat and mosquitoes in summer and the cold and snow in winter." She raised her arms in a large gesture. "And it's about this big, extended family that includes all the villagers. Love them or hate them, they're part of my life. Even Linda Wegner with her gossip. If I left, I'd miss her."

"No, you wouldn't," Sam said.

She laughed and heard the throb in her throat from leftover tears. "Maybe you're right. Maybe I don't know what I'd miss."

"There's only one way to find out."

A chill gust of wind blew into the barn, and she shivered. "Dad, you're the devil."

"Honey, you're not the first to say that."

THIRTY-SEVEN

E very day Katie thought about what her father said. Every day she thought of calling Gabe. Every day villagers called her or stopped her in the street with smiles on their faces, as if Santa Claus had come to town early and dropped off gifts that kept on giving. So excited that their stories were on YouTube. Wanting to know what she thought.

She lied, telling them how great they were, that talent agents from Los Angeles would fly to Miracle to sign them up. Making them laugh giddily, as if they harbored the hope that it might really happen.

In truth, she couldn't look at the videos. Afraid they hearing his voice would make her ache too much. It would make her miss him. Long for him.

Something miraculous happened when Gabe asked questions from behind the camera. He called something from people's souls that showed up on film.

On the second day Rosa called her, excitement in her voice, to tell her they had over $24,000 already.

"This is the miracle that was prophesied," Rosa said.

"It was Gabe," Katie said. "He's a magic man."

"I remember that song, and it wasn't money the singer was talking about. Are you in love with him?"

From outside the back door, Happy howled, wanting to come inside. Katie crossed to it. "He's good in bed."

Rosa laughed. "I would've guessed that. I'm glad you

had it with him. Do you want more?"

Katie opened the door and Happy trotted in. Except for the white on her face and her limping walk, no one would've known she wasn't a young dog. Happy was an old dog with a young attitude.

"To be with Gabe," Katie said, "I'd have to move out of Miracle."

"You could just have an affair. You could go to Chicago for a few days. Tony's saving for something he's not telling me about. He could use some extra money, and he knows his way around a kitchen. He could bake and deliver your pies. Leave the recipes you don't mind sharing."

It's not my recipes that make the difference, Katie thought, it's me.

"Other times," Rosa continued, "Gabe could come to Miracle and visit you."

"You make it sound easy. I do one thing, and he does the other. But I don't think it would work."

"Love isn't easy. It's messy." Rosa's voice was flat. "I take back all my advice. I'm the last person who should try to matchmake. I saw Amber at Wegner's this morning. She was wearing a maternity top."

"Bitch."

"She and Mike make a good pair. A bitch and a bastard. I think Tony's going to quit. He said he can't stand working with her still waitressing. Maybe that's why he's saving his money. To tide him over."

"He could get a job anywhere. Any restaurant owner in the county would snap him up."

"They would. But I don't know if cooking is his passion."

"What is his passion?"

"If he has one, he's not telling me." Rosa's voice was

sharp with worry.

Katie grimaced. It seemed everyone she knew had troubles except Happy. She'd already sniffed her dog dish just in case Katie had gone crazy and thrown in extra food while she was outside. Finding nothing there, she was lapping up her water. When that was done she would tour the floor in the cooking area to see if she missed any crumbs on her last tour.

No wonder she lived for so long. All the important chores she needed to do every day... She had responsibilities. Who would do them if she wasn't there?

"But this isn't about me," Rosa went on. "Back to you—"

"No." Katie snapped her attention back from Happy. Rosa wanted to worry about Katie because it would keep her from worrying about her sons and her own life. "I'm happy."

"You're a liar."

"I have a wonderful life."

"Maybe you do."

"I do." Katie imagined the words firm, like the bricks in Sam's fireplace. Firm like Rosa's will power—which was much stronger than Katie's.

It was hard fooling Rosa...and impossible to fool herself.

"Why is everyone trying to change my life?"

"Because we want to see you happy."

"I am."

"Okay. If you really mean it."

Katie laughed but heard the hysterical note in her voice. Her laugh stopped in a gusty inhale, and she said goodbye. She stepped out to Happy, scooped her up then headed toward the living room.

"Come on, baby. You know I don't need a man to be

happy, don't you? It's not because I'm afraid. It's because I know this will go away." She plopped onto the sofa, Happy on her lap. "I'll learn to be happy without him. After all, being happy is what everyone wants."

Happy pushed her ear against Katie's hand, saying without words, *Pet me right here.*

Obliging, Katie lowered her head and whispered into the floppy ear. "So why is it so hard to find happiness? And when we do, why is it so hard to hang onto it?"

The need to make a Mourning Pie hit Katie as she was about to go to bed. It would mean a loss of an hour's sleep, so she went to her bedroom, Happy bobbing along behind her. She could make the pie tomorrow morning.

But in bed every time she closed her eyes they immediately popped open. And her mind was wide awake though this was the same time she went to bed nearly every night. And it had been a busy day, as usual.

Finally she got out of bed and gathered the ingredients. Flour, sugar, butter, eggs, vanilla, milk and coconut.

It must be something in the coconut, she thought, that made it her Mourning Pie. She didn't know what it was, just that it worked.

It didn't take long to make it, but she had to stay awake while it baked. While she waited, she finally watched the videos Gabe had filmed. They were short, most under three minutes. She watched hers last and saw it had more than 20,000 views. Amazing.

She wanted badly to call Gabe. Instead she pressed the arrow to bring the video to life. As soon as her video image started to talk, she put her hands over her mouth. This was her second video, and she still felt odd watching herself.

When it was over, she brought her hands down. It hadn't been too bad. She had a great feeling about the way the village had come together. It was a good thing that they had done. It had changed the village—at least for a short time. People were smiling at each other like they were in Mayberry.

When the pie came out, it looked perfect. She set it on the counter to cool, sent silent prayers to whoever was going to get the pie, then shut down her laptop and went to bed where Happy was still snoring softly, not even aware that she'd gotten up.

As she lay down, she wondered for one second who was going to get the bad news. Not Trish, she thought fiercely, not her best friend.

Then she closed her eyes and that was the last thing she remembered before something woke her.

She lay stiff for a moment. It was usually dark when she woke up, but tonight it seemed darker. And it didn't feel right in her bedroom.

Slowly she turned her head to look at the clock with the red LED numbers. 2:19. Definitely not her normal wake up time.

Her heart pounded and she kept her breath shallow, the better to listen for any sounds that shouldn't be there.

Nothing. No footsteps, no breathing, no creaks.
No snoring.

Her heart breath caught and she rolled out of bed then stumbled to the light switch. *No, no, no. Not Happy.*

The snoring didn't mean anything, she told herself. Happy didn't snore all the time, just most of the time.

Katie blinked at the sudden light and hurried to

where Happy lay on her side in the corner. She knelt and put her hand on Happy's head. She was warm.

A breath of relief shuddered out, then she put her head closer to Happy's to drop a kiss on her head...and she didn't hear any breathing.

The *oh no* chorus in her head changed to *Please, God, let her live* as she slid her fingers under the loose folds of Happy's neck to feel for a pulse.

Nothing. There was no movement, no breathing, no heart beating.

Her knees dropped onto the short-napped carpet. Bending forward, she leaned her cheek against the back of Happy's head and sobbed.

THIRTY-EIGHT

"You look like hell." Sam waited in his back yard for Katie to reach him, the early morning sun showing the crags and valleys in his face. Behind him was the barn and behind that the cut fields. A ginger cat strolled out of the barn to give Katie a curious look. It turned away, not interested. After all, there were mice and squirrels to hunt this time of year. What human could compete with that?

Smart cat, Katie thought, then shifted her gaze back to her dad. "I feel like hell. Do you want pie?"

"You gave me two pies on Sunday."

"This is my coconut pie."

"Your Mourning Pie? Who died?"

Tears heated her eyes, but she kept staring at him. "Happy."

"Oh shit. I'm sorry, honey." He stepped forward and hugged her, holding her for a long moment. She closed her eyes and allowed herself to lean against him. To listen to the wind and the rustle of the leaves on the ground, an animal running through the yard. Somewhere a caw sounded. Crows. Vultures.

She pulled away from Sam, sniffing, her eyes damp, though she'd cried too much already this morning. "I'm sorry, too."

"She was old. It's amazing she lived this long." One side of his mouth kicked up slightly. "Maybe it's your pies. I always said that your pies are magic."

She smiled even as her eyes filled again. She'd only given Happy a few bites now and then, a few crumbs. Sweets weren't good for dogs, but eating was Happy's joy. And even with the occasional treat, she'd outlived every other dog that Katie had known.

"Will you bury her?" she asked, her voice thick. "By the apple trees? She really liked apples."

He nodded. "I'll do that first thing."

"And, Dad." She put her hand on his arm. "I'm going to Chicago."

"For how long?"

She shrugged. She didn't even know if Gabe wanted her there. She just knew that she wanted to be with him. There was an ache in her heart that wouldn't heal until she saw him. Kissed him. Held him.

She wanted Gabe to wrap his arms around her, hold her against him and whisper words of comfort in her ear. She wanted him to tell her that Happy was in heaven, waiting for her. As if he really was her angel and knew about dogs in heaven.

"What about your pies?" her dad asked.

"I called Tony. He's taking over for me. Rosa has the key to my house. I'm leaving my recipes and instructions. Everything I could think of."

"What will his dad say?"

"Tony doesn't care. He quit."

Sam nodded approval. "I bet Rosa's happy."

"I imagine she's not too upset."

Sam chuckled, and she smiled weakly. "I'm leaving my van. Tony will need it for deliveries. Can I borrow your car?"

He agreed, as she knew he would. She had uneven parents. One was the best in the world. The other was a stranger.

Maybe that was life, the good and the bad. Burying her dog was very, very bad.

"Did you call Gabe?" Sam asked.

She shook her head. She didn't know why the reluctance. Fear that he'd say no? Fear that she might get halfway there and not be able to drive the other half. The place she didn't even like to think of.

Her only good memories of Chicago were the ones of Gabe.

"He might not even be there. And then where will you be?"

"Chicago."

The furrows on his forehead deepened. "Call him."

She nodded and slowly walked to the house with the memories of her dead dog and her absent lover in every room.

Instead of picking up the phone, she stared at it. Maybe he was seeing someone else already. For all she knew, he might be with several women.

But the thought didn't make her want to run inside her house and make a Cheating Pie.

Then she remembered Happy's body, wrapped in her favorite blanket like a taco on the front porch. Happy always liked the front porch, especially on sunny days like today, with the rays of light shining down on her.

The thought of Happy and her resiliency, the way she plowed through life even in old age and never whined, the way she accepted each indignity—the arthritis, the cataracts, the loss of hearing—and kept on going, gave Katie strength. Her shoulders squared, she grabbed the phone and called Gabe. He picked up on the fourth ring.

"Katie," he said, his voice gravelly with sleep.

Immediately her eyes filled with tears and she turned

into a wuss.

Happy was a better dog than Katie was a woman.

"Happy died last night."

"Baby, I'm sorry." His voice was clear now. She pictured him sitting up in bed, swinging his legs over the side, a frown of concern on his face. The face she wanted badly to see in person.

She sniffed noisily. "I'm okay."

"You don't have to be brave. Not with me. I have two interviews this morning, but I'll leave right afterward. I'll cancel my appointments for tomorrow. I'll be at your place this afternoon."

Relief shuddered through her. But instead of assuaging her grief, it intensified. As if he'd given her permission to mourn. Hunching her shoulders, she rocked back and forth to keep from crying.

"Katie?"

"I'm here." Her voice came out high and wobbly. "I have a better idea. I'll drive to Chicago."

There was silence on the other end. Then he said one word. "Come."

THIRTY-NINE

Chicago was bright and shiny, and Chicago was dingy and dirty. Katie saw cars and buildings and stop signs and stop lights and traffic. Most of all there were roads. Highways, side roads, alleys, toll roads, expressways. She drove on a side street now, gripping the steering wheel and breathing shallowly, driving slowly to read the street signs. Something the man behind her didn't like, apparently, as he squealed past her dad's car.

Oh God, there was the sign for Gabe's street. She felt like a used dishcloth, but she turned the wheel and kept driving, looking anxiously at the addresses of the brick apartment buildings that lined the street. Toward the end of the block she saw a man standing on the sidewalk, looking her way. Was it—?

Yes! Her tight muscles relaxed, the tension seeping out. It was an effort to keep her spine straight as she searched for a parking spot. There weren't any, and she parked in front of a fire hydrant in front of the next building. Let Chicago fine her. Right now she didn't care.

In the rear view mirror, she saw Gabe stride away from the apartment building, a red brick rectangle that looked like an institutional building, not a place where people lived.

She opened the car door then hung onto it after she stepped out. Her legs were trembling. Her whole body trembled.

"Hey." Gabe held out his arms. "You made it."

She couldn't smile. Instead she fell into his open arms, closed her eyes and breathed him in. Being in his arms, feeling cherished, made the six-hour drive worthwhile. Even getting lost inside the city was worth it. Even though she'd called him three different times to guide her because monkeys had a better sense of direction than she did.

"You're shaking," he said.

"It will go away." She pushed back just far enough to look at him—his smiling blue eyes, his sweet, full lips, his nose that wasn't perfect and his wavy hair.

She reached up and curved her hand on his hair. "I'm with my angel now."

His grin widened, dimples creasing his cheeks. "If you knew my thoughts, you'd call me a very naughty angel. Let's park your car in the garage then get your stuff and go inside."

"There's a garage?" She allowed him to tug her back to the car.

"There's one space. Okay if I drive?"

"If I had to drive again today, I might want to shoot myself."

He headed toward the driver's seat while she hurried to the passenger side. Once inside, she asked, "You took your SUV out of the garage for me?"

"Don't worry, I expect to be compensated."

She smiled, not ready to laugh yet. "I brought apple pie."

"It's not pie I had in mind. Something more tasty." He turned the key and the engine purred.

Ten minutes later they stood in an apartment with furniture in shades of turquoise and fuchsia. On the wall were framed photos of different flowers. From where she stood, she could see the small kitchen.

"This isn't yours," she said.

"A friend is shooting a film in Canada, and she let me stay here. You don't like the colors?"

"I do. Just not on such a grand scale."

"It kind of hurts my eyes," he said. "But then I look at you and I'm healed."

She melted inside. Still sore at heart, still tired, but when she looked at him, it felt like the wrong tilt in the world had righted itself.

"Hungry?" he asked. "I have pizza. Do you remember Chicago pizza?"

"I remember being hungry often." She spoke slowly, the memories coming back in small pieces instead of the whole picture. She remembered being left alone and scared a lot, too, but didn't say it. Since she'd lived with her dad, she'd had a wonderful life. She wasn't going to feel sorry for herself.

He caressed the back of her head, his hand sliding over her hair. "I wish I lived somewhere else so you wouldn't have to relive the bad times."

She wanted to tell him that she was fine, but a wave of tiredness crashed down on her, and she closed her eyes and swayed. He gripped her arm, and her eyes snapped open.

"You need to lie down." His voice roughened with worry. "Alone. At least for now."

She couldn't even pretend to smile. The grief had hit her again. Hard. Happy had four legs and a tail, but that didn't mean Katie didn't mourn her. It didn't mean Happy deserved less than a person. After all, how many people loved as well and as unconditionally as a dog?

Gabe guided her to a decent-sized bedroom with a turquoise and purple bedspread that she imagined made

Gabe laugh when another guy would toss it on a chair, too feminine for him.

Right now it looked good to her. She kicked off her shoes then crawled beneath the cover. As she dropped her head on the pillow, it came to her that she could sleep now because she felt safe with Gabe. The man who could do no wrong.

He adjusted the cover around her neck. "While you're here, you could see your mother. It might be good for you."

Her eyes closed tight, she turned her head away from him.

He could do wrong after all.

FORTY

When she woke up the fading sunlight cast a golden glow on the turquoise and purple color scheme, and it felt like a world out of a fairy tale. Especially with Gabe smiling at her with warmth that heated her inside and out. He made her feel treasured.

She wasn't ready to go out and face reality and was glad when he ordered pizza. In twenty minutes the pizza was delivered, and they ate at the small dining room table. It only took one bite for Katie to agree that Chicago pizza was superior to Fabrini's. The red wine went down easily, but she limited herself to one glass.

"Ready for pie?" He gathered the plates, refusing her help, as if he knew she felt as if she were floating on a cloud. It was a great ride, but clouds were fragile. Unstable. Any moment she could fall off.

Right now, though, she wanted to enjoy the cloud.

But more than the cloud, she wanted to enjoy Gabe.

"I didn't come here for pie," she said. "I can have a piece later."

"Later?" His eyes sparked as if inside him a small fire burned.

She stood, and it was another part of the dream. A fantasy that was coming true.

She hoped not. She wanted the real thing.

"If you want your pie first..." She trailed off as he

stepped toward her.

His kiss was light at first. Tender. And for no reason, the tears started to fall even as she melted against him. Because she was melting inside, too.

"You're crying." His voice husky, he pulled away and wiped a tear from her cheek with his index finger, then put it in his mouth and licked it. "We'll do this another time."

"Now." She took his hand and pulled it to her. "We'll do it now." She put his index finger in her mouth and watched him as she sucked on his fingertip. Watched as the flame in his eyes burned brighter. Watched as he pulled his finger from her mouth. Watched as he put his arm around her shoulders and led her to the bedroom.

Inside the bedroom they undressed quickly. Knowing the drill. Clothes off. Loving on.

He kissed her, this time not gentle. Hard and fast before he put his arm around her and started toward the bed. She held back and hit the light switch.

"I want to watch you as we make love," she said.

Still holding onto her, he made a noise in his throat that sounded like a growl, and she laughed. Feeling strong again, with a hunger for him so great it made her want to devour him.

In his face she saw his tension, as if an inferno roared inside him. As if he burned for her as much as she hungered for him. Needed her as much as she needed him. To fill her. To love her.

Her body started to shake from all the need. It was too much. Too much for herself, and too much to put on any man.

She tried to pull back, but he wouldn't release her. They tumbled together onto the bed, and this man who was always so gentle was on top of her, holding her tightly, breathing harshly, pressing his erection against her.

Or was that her, holding him tightly, breathing harshly, wrapping her legs around him?

"Now," she said. "Now."

"Are you sure?" his voice ground out. Beneath her hands on his back, she felt his heated skin. Beneath her heels on his ass she left his tension. Beneath his erection, she felt as if she were going to fall apart.

"Now!"

He entered her. No foreplay needed. Small sounds came from both of them. She didn't know what came from who and she didn't care. This primal release, this satisfaction, this ecstasy, over and over again, was all she needed.

It seemed to last forever, her sensitive pulse points exploding with every in and out motion. She cried out and cried out and held on, her fingers digging into the backs of his upper arms.

And then it was his turn to cry out as he shuddered inside her and she let out a small scream, holding him even tighter.

He subsided on top of her, letting himself down slowly. Even in that most intense moment taking care of her.

His breathing was uneven and harsh in her ear as she thought, *I hope he doesn't say he loves me. It would be too much.*

He didn't say it. And neither did she. But they held onto each other as if they were the reincarnation of Romeo and Juliet, older and wiser, but still afraid someone was going to tear them apart.

And that story didn't have a happy ending.

FORTY-ONE

The hall light spilled into the bedroom and Gabe watched Katie sleep, still smelling like him. He probably smelled like her—like great, sweaty sex—and should shower, but he didn't move, not ready to leave her.

Love.

He wasn't ready for it, not now when he was just getting his life together, but it had come to him. He knew in Miracle that he loved her, but he'd left anyway. Now she was here, and all he could think was *How long before she leaves?*

Finally he got up, used the bathroom, cleaned the kitchen. Once that was done, he hesitated. Then he walked to the small office next to the bedroom. Close enough to hear Katie if she called out for him.

He needed to edit the videos he'd shot today and email them to the two sets of parents. He wanted to hold her all night, but he'd left Miracle to do these videos. Katie was here with him, but that hadn't changed.

She had her pie magic, and he...there was no magic in what he did, but there was a lot of heart.

These videos felt right. As if this was what he was supposed to do.

Being with Katie felt right, too. As if she was the one person in the world he would love completely.

Katie used to believe he was an angel. If that were so,

God was in heaven laughing at the trick he'd played,
giving him two loves that might split his heart in two.

FORTY-TWO

Katie looked less wan in the morning, more color in her cheeks. He'd done that with his lovemaking, he thought, even as he laughed at himself. As if he had a magic penis.

More likely it was the apple pie they were eating for breakfast.

"What does my pie make you think of?" she asked when they were done.

"Miracle."

Her eyes widened and she looked startled.

"What?" he asked.

She shook her head. "It's nothing."

"Tell me. What do you call this pie?"

"It's the Home Pie. When you eat it, you think of home."

He looked down at his plate, only crumbs left. She laid her hand lightly on his forearm, wordlessly calling his attention to her. He shifted his gaze to her face.

"Your pie is wrong."

Her eyelids lowered halfway down, closing off her thoughts from him.

"Miracle is a place for me to visit because you live there." He put his right hand over hers. "It will never be home for me. To do what I do, I need to be in a bigger city."

"Of course." She smiled with her lips but not her eyes.

He drew his hand from hers and she immediately slid hers off his arm.

He felt cold. Bereft. As if something had changed between them.

"Are you showing me your webisodes?" she asked, her voice bright.

"You still want to see them?"

She stood and leaned forward to kiss him. Her hair swung past his cheek and his ear, brushing his shoulder. Pulling back, she said, "That means yes."

He carried one of the dining table chairs into the office he'd set up a couple days ago in the second bedroom. It took him a minute to get the video up. So far he had filmed seven kids. She'd seen the first one, so he started with the second. As she watched, tears formed in her eyes to be driven away by a smile and even laughter that was soon drowned out by more tears.

When the last webisode was over, her hand was pressed over her mouth and she still stared at the screen where a bald twelve-year-old girl with no eyebrows smiled at them.

"These kids…" Her voice broke.

"I know." Emotion filled him, too. Pride for these videos. And for the kids he felt too much—too much pride, too much empathy. A good filmmaker was supposed to put something like this together with some distance. But when he filmed these kids there was no distance. Twenty-four years ago he'd been one of them, and it was a miracle that he was alive and making these films.

"My boyfriend is a genius," she said.

"Your boyfriend?" His lips curved up and he felt the smile all the way down to his toes.

"Can you think of a better word?"

"Lover."

She laughed and leaned toward him. They kissed, and his cell phone buzzed on the desktop. Still holding her, he picked it up and saw the name of a parent who'd said she needed to talk to her husband and would get back to him.

A weight settled in his chest. The real world was calling. "I have to take this."

She nodded and he walked into the kitchen and talked a few minutes, then called Taz. Taz had gotten a job with an indie director who was a stockbroker during the day and a filmmaker in the evening. Taz told Gabe the movie was about vampires and zombies in the Chicago Stock Exchange. His expression deadpan, Gabe said it might be too realistic to be fiction.

So far Taz was available during the day. Gabe felt as if everything was finally coming together for him.

Even the woman he loved had come to Chicago to be with him.

He didn't know why he felt like any moment a lightning bolt might strike him and rip apart his world.

After the arrangements were set he found Katie in the bathroom, brushing her teeth, the water running, door open. Even that everyday action seemed intimate. It made him want to call the mother of the boy with a brain tumor and see if he could come an hour later.

But that would be ridiculous. Besides, the mother had told him she had to be at work at 10 AM, so he needed to hustle.

"I have another interview."

She spit out the toothpaste and rinsed her mouth.

"I wanted to take you places today," he continued. "A walk on the pier. The art museum, the planetarium, the science museum..."

"All of that today?" She grabbed a washcloth and patted her mouth.

He laughed. "It would have to be a long day."

"Then there's no rush. Go do your interview and don't worry about me. I can drive to the lakefront and walk along it."

"You're sure?"

She rolled her eyes. He laughed and kissed her hard, tasting her peppermint-flavored toothpaste. She smiled at him, and when he was ready to leave, she was still smiling. He gave her his extra key and kissed her harder than usual. He had the crazy thought that he was imprinting his kiss on her.

Still smiling, she waved him off. When he got in his car that was cold from being left out all night, he had to fight a notion that he should go back to her. That she was like a bird, ready to fly away.

But that was his nerves talking. She just got here yesterday and wasn't going to fly anywhere soon.

FORTY-THREE

"Y̶ou should call your mother," Sam said. Holding her cell phone to her ear and looking at Gabe's computer for directions to the lakefront, Katie made a face. "She hasn't seen me since she dropped me off at the farm."

"She was an addict."

"Not anymore. She's had two kids since then and still hasn't shown any interest in seeing me."

"She keeps in touch."

"She calls once a year on my birthday. I dread those calls."

"Yet you still answer."

"Gram raised me not to be rude."

"Don't you want to know your half-sisters?"

She closed her eyes and bit down on her lower lip. Sam knew her too well.

"I'll call her."

"I'll give you her number."

"I'll get a pen." As she found one, she thought it was odd that she didn't know her mother's number. Not that it mattered. She'd only agreed to call her now because of Sam's prodding.

"Love you, honey," he said.

"Love you, too."

Feeling sick, she clicked the phone off. She hadn't even thought of her mother as she drove to Chicago.

Another oddity. And it was odd that she only remembered snatches of her childhood—and the clearest were about Gabe. He'd been her bright, shining angel. Other girls might have wished on stars or clapped for Tinkerbell. She had her own golden-haired angel.

And she still had him. Boy, did she have him.

Her mood lighter, she called her mother's number. As it rang, she walked to the front window. The apartment was on the third floor out of five. She looked out at a street with cars, SUVs and vans parked on both sides. Across the street were more apartment buildings that looked as if they'd been built in the 1950s, too. Not a picturesque view. On the corner was an Indian grocery store.

The phone rang again and then a third time. Katie's tense muscles relaxed. With the next ring it would go to voice mail and she wouldn't have to talk to her mother.

Instead a woman answered on the fourth ring. A stranger. Katie guessed it was Raelyn, but the voice never stuck in her mind. As if her mind rejected it the way her mother had rejected her.

"It's Katie," she said.

There was a pause on the other end, and Katie wondered if her mother knew other Katies and was trying to match the voice with the face.

"Your daughter."

"I knew that. I wondered why... Is something wrong? Sam? Is he all right?"

"I'm visiting a friend in Chicago. Dad suggested I call you."

"Did he?" Her tone wasn't pleased.

"I never met my half-sisters. How old are they now?" It dawned on Katie that she didn't know their birthdays. Why hadn't she asked before?

Probably because she never thought to ask. Her mother never liked talking about her half-sisters. Katie had found out because her grandmother had heard about them from an elderly relative of her mother's who lived in Tomahawk.

"Darling," Raelyn's tone turned coaxing, "I don't think it's a good idea for you to meet them."

"Really." Katie planted her feet apart. "Are you ashamed of them? Or of me?"

"It's not you, it's me."

"Are you kidding me? You're quoting the break-up line."

"No!" Raelyn's voice quivered. "It's really not you, and it's really not me, either. It's my husband. He doesn't want anyone to know what I was like before we were married. The children don't know they have an older sister."

Katie rocked back and forth on her heels, holding back a cry. "Why?" she asked, and her voice trembled. "Why did you contact me in the first place?"

"Your grandmother called and threatened me. Martin had just been accepted as principal of his first school. My aunt Lois in Tomahawk knew your grandmother and told her where I was. Your grandmother said if I didn't phone you at least once a year, she would write the school board and tell them that the man in charge of their children was married to a woman who abandoned hers. I *had* to call you."

"Then you should be happy. You'll never have to call me again." She hung up the phone and fought an urge to fling it across the room. With the first burst of anger burning inside her, she sucked in sobs. She would not cry over someone like her mother. Would. Not. Cry. Raelyn didn't matter to her. That was the last time she planned on talking to her.

Katie headed to the kitchen. She needed to make her Soothe the Soul Pie.

In the cupboards, she couldn't find ingredients besides sugar, flour and cinnamon. Not even butter, just margarine. She shuddered, then dug a pen and notebook out of her purse and started her list.

Feeling as though she were running on automatic, her emotions damped down until they were safe enough to pull out and examine—like hot coals cooling in a freezer—she put on her jacket, found the key, then left to shop at the Indian store on the corner.

Another time she would have stayed in the shop for an hour or more, smelling the spices with her eyes closed, asking the light brown-complexioned owners what was good with apple or pecan or even coconut. A thousand questions. But today she lingered only about twenty minutes. Though she'd seen cinnamon in the apartment, she didn't know how old it was, so she bought that and other ingredients, including a sugar pumpkin.

She hovered in front of the crystallized ginger. In the end, she bought a small bottle. This wouldn't be her soul soothing pie, but she hadn't been able to resist the pumpkin, smaller than the ones they grew at home. And like apple and coconut, pumpkin was a Comfort Pie. Just the smell of any of these pies baking in the oven always made her feel better.

In the next hour she cut the sugar pumpkin in half, scooped out the seeds, baked it and then puréed the pumpkin in a food processer.

She'd made pumpkin pie so often, once she found the food processor in a high cupboard, she did everything automatically, not even needing a recipe.

But as she poured the pumpkin mixture into a pie

plate, she couldn't shake off the feeling that something was wrong. Something was missing.

By the time the pie came out of the oven, she had watched The View, looked at the traffic out of the window and finished aerobic exercises that included jumping up and down as fast as she could to become breathless, proof that her heartbeat was speeding, her metabolism was up and calories were burning.

That meant she could eat two pieces of pie.

While the pie cooled she baked the pumpkin seeds then cleaned up and called Trish, who said she would never look at a pregnant dog from now on without empathy. She felt like she was carrying a football team inside her and they all wanted to be the team kicker. She couldn't wait until they were out of her.

Before Katie could say anything, Trish took it back. Of course she'd wait. Of course she'd do whatever was necessary to have healthy babies.

Katie agreed and wished she were back home so she could hug Trish.

But Miracle wasn't Gabe's home. Chicago was.

"How's your hunky blond boyfriend?" Trish asked, as if she were reading her mind. "I'm amazed you hooked up with someone from Chicago."

"I'm happy I can amaze you."

"So you're staying in Chicago? Or just a vacation?"

"I don't know."

"You love him?"

"I haven't told him yet."

"Then you do love him."

Katie closed her eyes. Her heart was still sore from Happy's passing. But when she thought of Gabe, her heart seemed fuller. Her whole body felt brighter.

"Yes."

"Does he love you?"

"I think so."

"It's been fast."

"Not all of us meet the love of our life when we're four."

"When I was four, I thought Gunner was a pest." Trish happily talked about Gunner and how he'd been the class nerd.

"But he was *your* class nerd," Katie said.

"True. Actually, Gabe was your angel, and you met him when you were five. So what do you think about that?"

The oven timer buzzed, giving Katie a reason to stop the conversation. She took out the pumpkin seeds and scraped them into a bowl sitting next to the pie. The pie looked beautiful, but as she gazed at it, her pie alarm rang. Something was wrong.

The smell. It wasn't right.

She backed away, her breaths short, her heart pounding.

This was nuts. The only thing wrong was her nerves. She needed to get out of here.

She was putting on her jacket when a key turned in the lock. One arm on, her jacket flapping against her thighs, she ran to the door. Gabe stepped in and she threw herself at him, holding him, hugging him, her head on his shoulder, tucked against the side of his neck.

FORTY-FOUR

Gabe hugged Katie back, feeling her heart pound against his chest. "What is it?"

She gulped in air and released it, repeating the process two more times, still holding onto him. Finally he no longer felt her heart slam and her breaths slowed to more normal inhales and exhales. Her grip eased, and she leaned back, looking into his eyes.

"I'm glad to see you."

"You sure that's it?"

"I'm turning into Happy," she said, stepping back, her eyes sad blue circles.

He looked at one side of her face, then the other. "It's too bad."

"What?"

"No droopy ears. Just think of the video I could put up on YouTube."

She laughed then stopped and blinked, as if surprised at the sound. "Idiot."

He smiled. If it stopped whatever the hell was scaring her, he'd play the idiot any day. "Don't I get a kiss?"

"Always," she said as they came together.

His lids closed, and an *ahhhh* hummed through him. It wasn't just her pies that were magic. Her kisses were another piece of magic.

When they parted, she smiled at him with her mouth and her eyes, and it felt to him as if her whole body smiled.

"A new fashion?" He nodded at her jacket that was half on, half off.

"I was about to go for that walk along Lake Michigan."

"I'll go with you. Won't be long." He headed to the office to put away his filming equipment. On his way out, he stopped to sniff the air. "I smell pumpkin pie."

She frowned. "It doesn't smell right."

"Smells great to me."

Opening the door into the hall, she grimaced. "Something is wrong. I don't know what it is."

"The ingredients? Were they stale? Maybe the oven is off. I never use it. It could be just the air in the kitchen."

"Chicago," she said quietly, so he strained to hear her. "I think it's the smell of Chicago."

She turned into the hall before he could reply. As he followed her, a sense of heaviness settled in his belly.

They took the stairs, no conversation between them. On the sidewalk, she glanced sideways at him. "I knew I forgot something."

He raised his eyebrows in a question.

She grinned. "My Packers sweatshirt."

Relief eased out the tension in his gut. "You can't wear that in Chicago. Packers fans are our mortal enemies."

"That means you're consorting with the enemy."

"Is that what you call what we've been doing? Consorting?"

"I like it. We can use it in a crowd of people and no one will know what we're talking about."

They both laughed. He slung his arm around her shoulders, and now it felt as if everything was all right in the world, though just a few moments ago everything had felt all wrong.

"How was the interview?" she asked.

"Good. The girl reminded me of you."

They got into his SUV and were on their way. It was early in the afternoon and the traffic should be fairly light to him, but he suspected it would seem busy to her. He turned east at the corner.

"How did she remind you of me?" she asked. "Was she tall and bony?"

"She said I was the angel Gabriel, and I would heal her."

There was silence for a moment. "In that case, I think she will heal."

He glanced at her. "If I could heal every kid just by being with them, I'd tour every damn hospital in the world."

She reached sideways and put her hand on his leg. "You don't know how powerful you are."

"Only when I'm consorting with you." He glanced quickly at her.

She smiled and pulled her hand back from his thigh. He immediately missed her touch.

Once they reached the walkway there was another switch of energy. It was parklike along the walkway, yet with a turn of their heads they could see tall buildings with long windows situated to catch the lake view. Another turn and they could see the sun sparkling on the water. The air smelled fresh, and the breeze had died down, perfect weather for a walk along a lake.

Other people thought this was a good day to stroll along the wide walkway, too, many of them with dogs. Katie stopped to pet every dog they saw, telling the owners about Happy.

The city of Chicago turned into a small town as they

sympathized with her and told her their dog stories, quite a few hugging her. Gabe left his card with a woman whose boss' son had cancerous tumor, and Katie told a seven-months-pregnant woman walking a poodle about her best friend being pregnant with quads.

After their walk he took Katie out for a late lunch. She'd told him how much she'd enjoyed the smells in the grocery store, so he took her to an Indian restaurant where she had the sampler plate and threatened him with her fork prongs when he swiped a piece of her tandoori chicken. When they were done, they refused dessert. Gabe told the waitress they had the best pumpkin pie in the world at home.

He turned with a smile to Katie and caught the small frown crossing her forehead. His smile dropped. He'd be glad when they were back at the apartment so they could eat the pie and discover it was delicious, like all her pies.

On their drive back to the apartment, the tension in the SUV thickened. He suggested a blues concert tonight, and she said she'd like that in a polite tone that had him clenching his teeth. He had to park his SUV on the next block. They walked to the apartment, hand in hand. But he felt a disconnect between them, a dissonance in the air.

Finally they were in the apartment, their jackets in the closet. Then she had to brush her teeth before she ate, saying she'd had too many spices to judge the pie. He brushed, too, because she was probably right, but he felt the tension building.

It seemed to take forever before they sat in front of the damn pie. He was starting to dislike it even before she served him a piece then dropped a large spoonful of whipped cream on it.

He took one bite and held back a groan. It was...good.

Nothing wrong with it. But it was a less flavorful version of her other pies. They'd tasted...luscious. Perfect. Amazing. This pie tasted about as good as his mother's, who never claimed to be a pie expert and just followed the recipe on the can.

"Delicious," he said.

"You're lying."

"It is good. Maybe it's the ingredients. Maybe they're old."

"Maybe I've lost my magic."

"There is no real magic. You're just a great pie maker. You have the touch."

"Yes, and the touch is called magic. Some people call it a miracle."

"Wasn't the miracle prophesied? But you were baking great pies long before—" He stopped. It had taken him too long to notice she was shaking her head, her mouth pressed in a grim line.

"It's Chicago." She pushed the plate away though she'd taken only three bites. "I think I can only do this at home."

"Katie..." He put his hand over hers on the table. She looked at him, her eyes dull as if a light had gone out of them. "That doesn't make sense. You had a shock. You're still grieving over Happy. Maybe some of the grief got in it."

"I made the apple pie after Happy passed. That had magic."

"It could be anything."

She nodded, but he could see she didn't believe it.

"You still want to go to the blues club tonight?"

"Sure." She gave him a smile with no joy in it.

At the club she appeared to enjoy herself, even laughing and talking, but it felt as if he had a stranger by his side. When they went to bed that night, he held her and she was stiff in his arms.

"I'm not going to make love to you," he said, his voice hoarse.

"I wouldn't mind."

"Shut up. Just shut up. Something is wrong, and I'm just going to hold you."

She gave one sob and turned her face to him, gripping him tightly.

"Thank you," she said. "I know I'm trouble. I know I'm a lot of work."

"It just so happens that my favorite kind of women are the ones who are a lot of work."

She huffed out a laugh. "You're an idiot."

"Yeah, but I'm *your* idiot."

"My angel idiot." She snuggled against him and relaxed her grip. He could tell when she fell asleep. He wondered what the next day would bring.

FORTY-FIVE

Katie pretended to be asleep the next morning until the door closed. Only then did she roll out of bed, feeling creaky and old. As if without her pie magic, her body had aged. She didn't know if it was because of Happy, her mom or her missing pie magic, but she felt like she'd gotten a triple whammy.

She had Gabe, she thought, turning on water for a shower.

But was he enough?

After her shower she headed to the kitchen. There was a cup of coffee in the unplugged coffee maker. She warmed it in the microwave and was sipping it when her cell phone rang. Her father's name was on the display, and she put it to her ear. Sam didn't normally call to chat. Of course, she normally lived next door to him.

"Hi, Dad. Is everything okay?"

"Trish just went to the hospital in Tomahawk."

"Oh no. The babies aren't due for seven weeks. Trish said they might come earlier, but I was hoping they'd have more time. At least they kept up their insurance."

"Insurance doesn't pay for everything. I'm bringing a box of Kleenex. I hear hospitals charge for that. Next they'll charge for toilet paper. When anything happens, I'll call you—"

She headed for the bedroom, the phone to her ear. "I'm coming home."

"With Gabe?"

"He has work to do here. I don't."

"Baby—"

"I can't talk about it now. I have to pack. I'll be there in about six hours. Love you."

"Love you, too."

As she packed, she thought of the letter she would write Gabe. She couldn't call him. If she did, he might tell her that he would come with her, and she'd have to tell him to stay.

Because the truth was, once she got home, she doubted if she could go away again. It was the coward's way out to write a letter, and she guessed that made her a coward. She could live with that.

What she couldn't live with was the loss of her magic. It was like living in the world where there was no sun. Just a dim haze.

It was either Gabe in Chicago or her pie magic in Miracle. There were win-win situations, and this was a lose-lose.

Perhaps she should give it more of a chance, but right now leaving felt like the right thing to do.

I love you, she wrote at the end of the letter. *Chicago is a wonderful city, but Miracle is my home.*

Don't come for me.

Love,

Katie

Twenty minutes later she managed to navigate her way out of Chicago without getting lost once. Proof that she was doing the right thing.

But if that were so, why did her eyes burn with unshed tears? And why did she feel a little dead inside?

Her heart had ached coming to Chicago. It ached even more leaving it.

FORTY-SIX

Gabe drove through Chicago with an overdose of sadness. Today's shoot had been rotten lousy sad. The six-year-old girl he'd filmed should grow up to be vibrant and passionate like her mother and tall like her father. Should have friends, lovers, and adventures. Maybe a husband and children.

None of that was going to happen.

On the video she said she was happy that her story would help other children.

It hadn't been easy smiling at her and nodding while he wanted to yell at the sky and demand to know why things like this were happening.

He was glad to be home. There was even a parking spot right in front of the building. A sign that his day was going to get better.

Once inside the apartment building, he felt a tension. A worry he couldn't shake off. He wanted to run up the three flights, but the equipment hanging from his shoulders didn't take well to running. The elevator seemed to take longer than usual, the slowest elevator in the world. When it reached the third floor, he burst out, surprising another neighbor, a fiftyish woman who squeaked. He normally would apologize, but the feeling that something was wrong wouldn't allow it.

He reached the apartment and, clumsy with worry, it took him three tries to get the key in right.

"Katie!" he called, rushing inside. "Katie!"

No one answered. No one came. He stopped in the living room. Breathed in, and in that one inhale, he knew Katie wasn't there. He didn't smell her, he didn't feel her. The apartment felt empty, like a body without a heartbeat.

Throwing his equipment on a chair, he called out her name again anyway. Without waiting for a reply, he headed to the bedroom. The door was open, the bed made. No Katie.

From there he strode to the office, passing the bathroom with the door open. No Katie either place. Maybe she'd gone for a walk. Maybe she was going to make another pie to see if yesterday's was a fluke.

Only the kitchen was left and he hurried toward it. But something niggled in the back of his mind, and when he entered the kitchen, he knew what it was.

There had been no suitcases in the bedroom.

A note lay on the table, the paper lines and torn out of the notebook on his desk.

Dread settled over him like a gray cloud. He tottered toward the notebook, his legs and feet reluctant. He knew even before he looked at it what it was going to say.

Goodbye. Sayonora. Nice knowing you.

It's just not working for me. I can't do this.

He picked it up. Her words were phrased more politely, including the information about her friend. But if she'd left because of her friend, she would have come back as soon as she was well again. Her pie magic was the real reason she wasn't coming back.

He'd left her for his videos. Now she was leaving him for her pies.

Karma was kicking his ass.

I need you, Katie, he thought. *I need you now. And*

you aren't here for me.

He crumpled the note in his fist, laid his head on the table and remained like that for long moments.

His heart hurt. His soul was dark. A light inside him turned off.

Finally he stood, opened the liquor cabinet, looked at the bottles for a long time then closed it. In the note, Katie said not to come after her, but he wasn't letting her go. There had to be some way they could fix this. A way they could be together and be happy.

His steps purposeful, he headed to the bedroom to pack. He had a six hour drive ahead of him.

FORTY-SEVEN

It was dark when Katie made it to the hospital, and memories swirled back to her of visiting Gabe in the first hospital she'd been to all those years ago, her little heart pounding in her chest. Only her surety that Gabe was an angel and would not die gave her the courage her go inside and talk to him.

She felt the same reluctance now. What she didn't have was the same certainty. Instead she just had a pounding in her gut that something was wrong. That Trish needed her.

The nurse on the maternity ward told her she should go to the waiting room, nodding at the way she'd come as she picked up a phone then turned partially away. Katie hurried back, telling herself the nurse's dismissal was a good sign. Surely the lack of empathy meant nothing was horribly wrong.

When she entered the room, on one end she saw a group of people she didn't know. On the other end she spotted Sam with Reverend Elsa, a slender blond woman in her fifties who'd come to Miracle three years ago and founded the Church of Radiance. A *feel good* church, Sam called it with an indulgent smile. He had nothing against anyone feeling good and Katie suspected neither did God.

Sam and Elsa sat on a small sofa, leaning toward one another, as if they didn't want anyone else to hear what

236

they were saying. Katie hurried toward them, and Sam glanced up and stood.

Katie ran to him, her arms out, just the way she'd done many times as an anxious child. He caught her now as he did then, hugging her.

"Daddy," she pushed away, still feeling the comfort of his arms and solid chest, "is Trish—?"

"She'll be okay," he said. "The doctors did a cesarean four hours ago. I was just about to leave. I offered Trish and Gunner my house until they can build theirs, but Elsa already offered." He gave the blond woman an admiring look, and she smiled back at him, straight into his eyes, in a way that made Katie suspect the admiration was mutual. Sam was probably about ten years older than Elsa, but with his long face and still firm jaw he'd aged well.

Katie had seen a lot of women look at Sam that way when she was growing up. If she was right about the vibration she was picking up, she felt sorry for Elsa. Her father was an easygoing guy, but he had strong feelings. The strongest were for an old love who was married to another guy. Not Katie's mother, but someone whose name Katie never knew. Though she'd only talked to Elsa a handful of times, Katie liked her enough to hope she didn't get too involved with her dad.

His heart was taken. His body...well, that was a matter Katie preferred to ignore.

"How are the babies?" Katie asked. Despite the nurse's lack of emotion, the feeling that something was wrong still had a stranglehold on her heart.

Elsa and Sam shared an *oh shit* look, and Katie's gut twisted harder. She clenched her jaw, ready for the worst.

When Sam turned to her, his expression was serious.

"Three babies are in incubators. They're around three pounds, but the doctor thinks they'll be okay."

"*Thinks?*" Katie didn't like that word. She liked *is sure* better.

"You know how doctors talk. They don't like to say yes or no. They aren't God."

"If three are in incubators," Katie said, turning to Elsa for answers, "and one is in the regular nursery, why is my dad frowning?"

Elsa clasped Katie's upper arm as if she needed to support Katie. Which was ridiculous, as Katie was about five inches taller than Elsa and certainly outweighed her. "I'm sorry," Elsa said. "A little girl didn't make it."

Katie rocked back on her heels, holding back a cry. She felt a burn of sorrow for Trish, Gunner and the little one that didn't make it.

"At least Trish was nearly seven months along," Elsa continued. "That makes a difference in the babies' development."

"You're sure Trish is okay?" Katie asked. "The nurse said she couldn't see me now."

"She's sleeping," Elsa said. "She's worn out. Gunner went home to be with the two boys."

"Everyone else left," Sam said. "We knew you were coming and waited for you."

Katie wondered what he meant by *we*. It almost sounds as if... She shut down these thoughts, too wiped out emotionally to speculate. She used to dread her father hooking up with a woman. Now she wished he would.

It was time for him to get over that long ago lover. She trusted that he would choose someone who was...well, good.

Like Rosa, maybe. He was a little old for her, though

he seemed younger. But right now that wasn't Katie's concern. Her concern was... A wave of tiredness stopped her thoughts and she swayed slightly. Her mind was hopping all over the place, trying not to think of the dead baby.

Trying not to think of Gabe.

Sam put his hand on her back. "You need to go home and sleep. Don't worry about Trish and the babies." He glanced at Elsa. His mouth didn't smile but his eyes did. "Elsa put a glow of health and well-being around them."

Elsa patted Katie's back. "I give great glow."

Just from her touch, Katie felt a little glow and a little comfort. Maybe one of these Sundays she would attend a service at Elsa's church.

"Come on, Katie, let's go home." Sam nodded at Elsa. "Thanks for staying while I waited for my girl."

Elsa smiled and nodded, but her eyes held sorrow.

Inside Katie, something stirred, an urge she'd thought was dead.

"What's wrong?" Sam asked.

Katie shook her head because nothing was wrong. Something was right. Looking at Elsa, she felt an urge to bake her a Sad Pie.

Her nerve ends shimmered, and she stopped herself from leaping forward and kissing Elsa, then laughing out loud.

Her pie magic was back.

"You sure nothing's wrong?" he asked.

"I'm just tired."

"You look beat," Sam said. "I'll drive you home."

"I can drive myself. I'd have to leave your car here and—"

"I'll drive you back tomorrow." Sam's voice left no room for denial. "I've got some of Rosa's lasagna in my freezer. I'll warm a plate up for you."

"Dad, you're the best." She hugged him, then let go and smiled up at him, feeling teary again. Gazing at him, a thought came into her head: *Gabe would be a father like that.*

"Something wrong?" he asked.

"Nothing." Except for the dazed feeling, as if she'd walked into a thick glass door. "If I can't see Trish, I'd like to see the babies at least."

Elsa led them to the nursery. Two nurses greeted her on the way, and it was apparent she'd been there before. Katie didn't know how often, but she suspected Elsa would be hard to forget.

She stopped in front of a set of clear windows where they could see five babies in incubators. So tiny and skinny with breathing tubes wrapped around their heads. They were too far away to see their features clearly. Katie felt for the babies, and she ached to pick them up. She could imagine how Trish and Gunner must hurt.

They left a moment later, Elsa and Sam chatting about Becky, the former minister's wife who was pregnant. According to Linda Wegner, Becky and the baby's father wanted to get married now.

Sorrow swept over Katie with all the baby news. There would never be a baby of hers and Gabe's. She had her home and her pies, but she didn't have Gabe.

FORTY-EIGHT

Gabe's car idled on the road in front of Katie's cottage as he stared at the dark shape of her house. There were no streetlights at this end of the road. There was only her house and Sam's, which was dark, too. There was no moon, either, and he thought it possible she didn't lock her back door. That he could go to her house and walk in.

If she was sleeping, she might not even hear him. He could take off his clothes. Lie in bed with her. Close his eyes and know he could go to sleep breathing the same air as her.

He could see it in his mind...

Or he could see another scenario...

Katie waking up, hearing an intruder in her house and grabbing a baseball bat.

Or a shotgun. He didn't know if she had one, but this was not the best way to find out.

Even if he did it and she didn't scream—if she in fact slept until morning and they had breakfast together— what would he say to her? His situation hadn't changed. He couldn't do what he loved while he lived in Miracle. It was just too...small.

He sat for a moment longer, a fifty-pound weight in the pit of his stomach. Finally he steered the SUV in a U-turn and headed to Tomahawk where he would find something to eat and a room for the night.

A half hour later he sat in a Chinese restaurant with decent food. He even drank a Tsingtao beer, which wasn't bad. At a motel room he set up his latest video to see what he could edit. But it hurt to look at the small girl's pale face and courageous smile, knowing she was likely going to be dead soon.

Too young. Too damn young.

When he finally went to bed alone, he couldn't sleep for a long time, thinking of Katie. Aching for her.

He felt defeated. Hopeless.

There had to be something he could do. Some way to fix this. But his mind was blank and his heart already mourning. As if it knew there was going to be no happy ending.

FORTY-NINE

The next day the sun shone dimly through thick, gray clouds, and the radio DJ predicted rain. A portent, though Gabe believed less in portents than angels. But when he reached Katie's house, she either wasn't home or wasn't answering the door.

He drove back to Tomahawk. He hadn't called last night or this morning. As if expecting her to be there for him all the time. He could call her now but decided against it. She would probably go to the hospital when visiting hours opened at 11 AM. He'd see her then.

He found a diner he remembered being not too bad. As he ate his eggs and toast, something niggled in his brain. It felt important, but the more he tried to catch it and examine it, the more it slipped out of his reach.

The waitress refilled his coffee, and he thanked her, not even glancing at her. Still busy trying to catch that—

"Gabe? Mind if I sit down?"

He glanced up into the attractive face of an older blond woman who looked vaguely familiar. "Sure, have a seat. Glad to have company."

Her left eyebrow rose, sending her doubts to him. "I doubt that, but I'll sit anyway. I didn't realize it would be this crowded."

Peering behind her, he saw that the diner was full. "Neither did I." He wasn't noticing a lot of things these days. Like how unhappy Katie had been in Chicago.

"We were never introduced. I'm Elsa Hahn." She held out her hand.

Taking it, he felt a current of energy and was glad when the handshake was over. "Nice to see you again, Reverend Elsa."

"Ah, you did remember."

"I think someone said you're the minister that doesn't believe in Jesus."

"I do believe there was a Jesus. A nice Jewish boy who was smart and charismatic with a wonderful heart." She tilted her head and studied him, her eyebrows drawn together. "You look...sad. I sometimes connect to people. I can't read your mind, but I'm good at reading emotions."

He shrugged. "Body language."

"As good an explanation as any. In your case, I can see that you're carrying a lot of weight on your shoulders."

He shook his head. "Not really. I'm doing something that fulfills me."

"Perhaps, but that doesn't mean it's a light load." Her eyes looked far away for a moment, giving him a freakish feeling that he could reach out to where she sat and touch air. "I think what you're doing is important. It doesn't just fulfill you, it fulfills many people."

He felt stunned, his breath stuck in his throat. Her words too much right now. He felt like bolting.

She blinked, as if she'd traveled back to the diner from whatever dimension her mind had gone. "I scared you. I didn't mean to."

"Not at all," he said, an automatic denial, though she scared the hell out of him. "It's more grandiose and bigger than I've been thinking, but I wouldn't mind if you're right."

"I usually am." She smiled sadly and leaned forward as if to share a secret. "But I can't tell you how socially awkward it is."

He laughed as the waitress brought her tea. "How's Trish doing?" he asked. "And the babies?"

"Trish is recovering. One of the babies didn't make it."

He winced, and she reached across and squeezed his hand. "You were a big help. What you and the villagers did was something special. And everyone who shared money or good wishes. To have that many people help them was empowering. The work on their new house is already started. We want to get it done before it snows."

He winced again, and she made a face. "It's that time of year, though with global warming..." She raised her eyebrows, her expression resigned yet smiling. "I've been following your videos of the children with cancer. They're heartbreaking and brilliant. And often inspirational. I believe anyone who watches them will want to be a better person. I know I do."

"I'm glad you got that. I always wanted to tell stories that would rivet people, shock or awe them. Be so powerful it would change lives." He stopped and scratched his neck behind his ear. "That kind of sounds like I want to be God."

She reached out and touched his hand for a second, and he breathed easier, as if her touch infused comfort into him. "We're all pieces of the higher power," she said. "The universe. God. Yahweh. Whatever you want to call it."

"So we're all one big Yahweh puzzle?"

Her eyes glowed with gentle humor. "That's humanity for you. We keep finding the pieces that fit."

"I'm not having too much luck with that lately. I wish

your higher power would show me where some of the pieces are hiding."

"Or give you a kick in the ass."

He half smiled. "If that's what it takes. Right now I feel like I belong to two puzzles instead of one. And if I go with one, I'll miss the other."

"It will come to you. We have miracles happen in our village."

"Twenty-three years ago, my doctors said I was a miracle because I was alive. I have the impression that Yahweh isn't going to fix me again. This time I need to fix myself, and I don't know how to do it."

"There's no middle road?"

"I thought we were talking about puzzles, not maps." He shook his head before she could reply. "Never mind. Neither way works."

"You're sure?"

He looked her straight in the eyes and quietly said, "My heart is bleeding."

As he said that, something happened. It felt as if the room shifted. He didn't hear silverware knocking together or glasses falling and breaking, but something made him look up at the door opening for another diner.

At first he didn't see anyone, just the open door. A movement sent his gaze downward to a child entering the diner. Nothing exceptional about that, but this child wore a cap and was bald.

His first thought was *Not again. Not now.*

And then came the second thought. That either through Yahweh or fate or just by dumb luck, he'd found another piece of the puzzle.

FIFTY

H *e was here.*
　　　Katie watched Gabe stroll into the waiting room with Gunner, and it felt to her as if the room brightened. Her heart knocked against her chest wall. She stood slowly while the other twenty or so friends, neighbors and gossips remained sitting.

"Hey, everyone," Gunner called. "The doc's happy with the babies' progress. He thinks they'll be in the NICU for at least a few weeks, but he says they're fighters. Not sure how we'll feel about that when they're older, all fighting for the same toy, but now it's a good thing."

Everyone spoke at once, assuring Gunner that it was a good thing. Gunner held up his hand until the voices died down.

"Another good thing is that we're starting to build the new home while they're safe in their incubators." He gestured to Gabe. "And here's the guy who's making our new home happen."

Another wall of voices rose. Katie thought she was the only one not talking. She couldn't talk, her voice stuck in her throat as she stared at Gabe. In his charcoal turtleneck and black jeans, Gabe looked yummier to her than any pie she'd made. She wanted to taste him, taking little bites that didn't hurt up and down his body.

It wasn't right for him to follow her to Wisconsin.

It wasn't right for him to look so delicious.

Putting his hands up, warding off the praise, Gabe laughed. "It's not me. It's thanks to everyone involved. And it's thanks to everyone who sent a contribution whether they live in India or Indiana."

Everyone got to their feet, clamoring to talk to him. Everyone except Katie. She sank back into her chair, her knees feeling like the bendy part of straws. Gabe went around the room, starting with the person furthest from Katie. He treated every person as if they mattered. As if they were important. He noticed things about people. He seemed to care.

No wonder they treated him like he was royalty, saying a few words to him, then sitting down with a silly smile while he moved on to the next person.

Ridiculous, she thought. But the nearer he came to her, the shorter her breaths grew.

He finally reached the person next to her, Becky, who'd been telling Katie about her wedding plans. She kept touching her belly as if to make sure the baby was all right.

"May I?" Gabe glanced at Becky's belly.

She laughed. "Why not? Everyone else does."

Instead of just touching her stomach, he bent so that his mouth was an inch from her belly. He whispered, "Grow strong, grow tall, grow wise."

"That's so beautiful," Becky said as he straightened. She stood and hugged him. "Thank you."

"It's my pleasure." He smiled at her and then stepped in front of Katie.

She could barely breathe. Gabe didn't say anything at first. Just took her hands and tugged. Slowly she stood. "I have to go now," he said.

"Of course." The words dragged out of her even as she

silently cursed him for coming. Cursed him for charming the whole room. Cursed him for making her love him even more.

He dropped her hands then turned and walked out of the room, taking with him the tiny bit of hope that maybe he'd come for her. That maybe he'd found a way to make it happen.

But it was never going to happen. Ever.

Katie's pie magic wasn't letting her brood. She was making this pie in a frenzy, *knowing* she needed to make her Everything Will be All Right pie. The emotion possessed her, as strong as if someone were holding a gun to her head. Stronger, because it came from her soul. As if pies came from the soul. The two crusts, life and death. The filling. Everything in between. The sugar and the spices. And in this case, bourbon and walnut.

Finally it was in the oven and she collapsed on the sofa and started to drift off. Trusting that the oven alarm would wake her, she let the sadness sneak back in, let it drain her energy. The sadness wasn't part of her pies. Sad and pies didn't go together. But that was what she felt now.

Love sucked. Before this whirlwind of emotions smashed into her, she was content with life. From now on, she would feel as if she were missing a part of her soul. Like pumpkin pie without the cinnamon and ginger.

She'd been up since 4:00 AM baking her pies, then she'd chased to Tomahawk to replenish her supplies, and after that she'd gone to the hospital to see Trish and Gunner and the babies and their many visitors. Alone in her house now, she thought that Trish's life was overflowing with babies, and hers felt empty. She didn't even have a dog anymore.

She drifted off to sleep as she admitted to herself that she was still grieving for Happy. Though Gabe was alive, nothing had changed and she grieved for him, too.

The oven alarm woke Katie. She was in the kitchen before it rang again, her mind still fuzzy with sleep. She took out her perfect pie, put it on the counter to cool, then stumbled back to the sofa.

The second time she was awakened, it was by a kiss. She jerked upright, her forehead hitting Gabe's.

"Ow," they said at the same time, pressing their hands against their foreheads.

"You're not Sleeping Beauty," he said.

"Not unless she has flour beneath her fingernails." She twisted so she was sitting, sliding her legs over the side of the sofa.

"Your face, too." He rubbed his index finger against her cheek.

"What are you doing here? I told you not to come after me."

"I read the letter, but you didn't say the one thing that would keep me away." His smile held sadness. "That you don't love me."

She opened her mouth and tried to say it...but the words wouldn't come out, her vocal chords frozen, her mouth refusing to open.

"It won't work," she finally said, her vocal chords unfreezing, though the coldness remained in her chest and her heart. "We'll be miserable."

"We can make it work. I have plans. I already set up my own channel. My videos are still on YouTube, but viewers can go direct to my channel, too. I want to give away a portion of the proceeds from the kids' videos to the cancer research foundation. I want to grow as a brand, and I believe I can do it. No one else is doing what I do."

"I believe you'll be a success, but that doesn't change anything for us. I liked Chicago, but I can't live there."

He sat on the sofa next to her. "Chicago isn't the only place where kids have cancer. Unfortunately it's all over."

"But your contacts are in Chicago. Your—"

His hand on her thigh stopped her words and her breath. The laughter in his eyes started her breathing again. "There's a children's hospital with pediatric cancer care about an hour and twenty minutes from Miracle."

"That's a long drive."

"I just came from there, and compared to what these kids are going through, I don't mind a drive. And look what I get to come home to. I'll smile all the way there and all the way home. I'll be living my dream, and I'm a damn lucky guy."

Hope grew in her. Hope and fear, because she wanted it so badly. Wanting something so big and so wonderful had risks. Risks that her heart would break again.

"What if your dream changes?"

"My dreams may change. My love for you...that's just going to grow." He leaned closer to her, his voice low and intense. "For years I've said my other passions—or lack of them—kept me from a serious relationship, but now I think all along I was waiting for you. You're my miracle. Will you marry me?"

"*Marry?*" She stared at him. She'd expected him to ask her to live with him. And despite her fears, she'd say yes... But marry? "It's so soon."

"Not soon at all." He smiled slowly, dimples

indenting, eyes shining in the way that made her spirits lift, as if all was right with the world. "We've known each other for twenty-three years. That's a long time to wait to get married."

She laughed, her breath hitching, filled with so much joy she could feel it flying out of her, into the world, the air, sparks of happiness. "Yes. You're my angel." She put her hand on the side of his face. "And sometimes you're my devil. I love you."

He reached for her, and this kiss was different from any other. Tenderness mixed with passion and hope and love.

"I suppose you're going to make a pie about this," he said, his voice husky.

"I already did." She was smiling so widely her face hurt. "We can have a piece after we make love."

"First I have something for you. An engagement present." He pulled away from her and stood. "It's at your dad's."

"I'd rather have you than a present," she said, but stood and followed him to the back door. Curious and a little uncertain. A new mixer maybe? The one she had was about twelve years old. It was about time—

He opened the back door, and a yip stopped her thoughts. A puppy's version of a bark.

"You didn't," she said, but he was stepping outside. "It's too soon. It's—"

The yip turned into a howl. Not a full adult Beagle howl, but a baby Beagle howl.

Her breath caught, and she stepped out. It was too soon. Way too soon. But the small, thin, short-legged, floppy-eared puppy scampered toward them, falling twice along the way. Tripping over its puppy legs. And each time getting up again.

"Oh," she said. "Oh." As if the puppy knew she was talking to it, it ran toward her, its ears flapping, eyes bright brown and healthy.

"You're crazy." She kissed Gabe, fast and hard. "A crazy man."

"Crazy in love with you."

Laughing, she stooped down and held out her arms to catch the puppy and let it lick her face, feeling an instant bond.

She didn't know the puppy's sex but knew what she was going to name it.

Miracle.

Acknowledgments

Five smart, funny and talented writers helped make my book about pies, love and miracle better: Dale Mayer, whose dedication and talent inspires me. Michelle Diener and Liz Kreger, who ask all the right questions. Misty Evans, with her magic touch and generous soul. Sally Berneathy, for her encouragement and editing expertise.

I dedicate this book to my mother, who instilled in me a love of books and pies. And to Rose, the small Beagle with a big heart.

About Edie Ramer

Edie Ramer is funnier on the page than in real life. A multiple award-winning writer, she writes stories with heart, attitude, and magic. She lives in southeastern Wisconsin with her husband, dog and one important cat.

Connect with Edie Online

www.edieramer.com
https://twitter.com/edieramer
http://www.facebook.com/edieramer.author